FERRET
ISLAND

A rollicking adventure
for brave young readers

FERRET
ISLAND

Richard W. Jennings

Houghton Mifflin Company Boston 2007

Walter Lorraine Books

Walter Lorraine (*wr*) Books

www.houghtonmifflinbooks.com

Library of Congress Cataloging-in-Publication Data
Jennings, Richard W. (Richard Walker), 1945–
  Ferret Island / Richard W. Jennings.
       p. cm.
     "Walter Lorraine books."
  Summary: Stranded on an island in the middle of the Mississippi
River, fourteen-year-old Will Finn discovers a race of giant ferrets and
a reclusive author who plans to use the animals in a plot against
McDonald's.
  ISBN-13: 978-0-618-80632-4
  ISBN-10: 0-618-80632-6
  [1. Islands—Fiction. 2. Ferrets—Fiction. 3. Adventure and
adventurers—Fiction. 4. Mississippi River—Fiction.] I. Title.
  PZ7.J4298765Fer 2007
  [Fic]—dc22
                                                    2006036329

Printed in the United States of America
MP   10   9   8   7   6   5   4   3   2   1

For Vivien Bolen Jennings

Author's Note:

This story appeared in slightly different form
in fifty-one weekly installments in 2005–6
in *Star Magazine*, the Sunday magazine of
The Kansas City Star,
Tim Janicke, editor.

All I wanted was to go somewhere.
All I wanted was a change.
I warn't particular.

—Mark Twain,
The Adventures of Huckleberry Finn

FERRET ISLAND

A Freak of Nature

Perhaps if our brains were larger we could understand nature's grand plan, but what I've seen of the world so far seems like a series of unsuccessful experiments, with no species holding the upper hand forever.

Marine invertebrates, giant reptiles, packs of apes—all have had their shot at running things on earth, and failed. And from the latest evidence, it appears that our days may be numbered, too.

So who's next in nature's line of succession?

Some scientists say it will be microbes. Others predict that once man has eliminated himself, cockroaches will rule. A few dreamers are hoping for the arrival of kindly visitors from outer space. To my way of thinking, they're all wrong. Because with nature, the one thing you can always count on is a surprise.

One such surprise arose in the Mississippi River on a backwater sandbar formed by an oxbow some seventy miles south of Memphis. For years, despite being within earshot of around-the-clock barge traffic, the weedy little island managed to escape all human habitation.

It was less successful at avoiding a pair of displaced household pets.

In 1957, in the middle of the night, two domesticated ferrets (whose names were Snowball and Louise), clinging to a warped kitchen table sent southward by the spring floods from a farmhouse near the little river town of Kennett, Missouri, were deposited by the swirling water onto the sandbar.

Right away, under a pale yellow moon, the two soggy weasels set up housekeeping.

Like the achievement of Adam and Eve, the origin of weasel life on the island occurred many years before I was born. Indeed, it wasn't until 1990 that I drew my first breath in a hospital delivery room in Kansas City, Missouri, and it was 2004 before fate, circumstances, and my own bad temper took me to this strange hidden land that time forgot.

Running away from home is always a mistake, but I had no intention of being gone for good. Yet before I fully appreciated what I'd done, I was on a smelly, diesel-powered Greyhound bus headed east on a crowded interstate highway filled with potholes.

Ah, the open road! As the barn-dotted landscape zips by, every strange sound, pungent smell, and whispered conversation hints at adventure. Until you get hungry, that is, which for me was less than an hour after the bus pulled away from the station.

What an idiot I am, I thought. *Why didn't I have the foresight to bring an apple, or string cheese, or a Snickers bar?*

All I had in my backpack was a change of clothes, a toothbrush, and a book by the celebrated author Daschell Potts.

In St. Louis, I transferred to a bus bound for Memphis, Tennessee, where my stepgrandmother lives, taking a seat beside a woman who reminded me of my sixth grade guidance counselor.

Kind-looking, sweet-smelling, and packing a loaf of zucchini bread that she insisted on sharing, the guidance counselor look-alike introduced herself as Miss Foster, a dance instructor from St. Charles, Missouri, en route to her great-uncle's funeral in Yazoo City, Mississippi.

"He was a brilliant man," Miss Foster told me. "He invented the McDonald's Happy Meal."

"Wow," I said, impressed. "Your great-uncle invented hamburgers, fries, and a small Coca-Cola?"

"Oh, goodness, no," Miss Foster corrected me. "They already had those."

"Oh," I said. "So he invented the prizes."

"No," she replied. "Those came later from factories working around the clock in Taiwan."

"I get it," I said, nodding. "Your great-uncle came up with the pictures for the box."

"Well, not exactly," Miss Foster said. "The first designs were suggested by three young men in Cleveland whose names were Eric, Billy Joe, and Dick."

"But if he didn't think up the food, the drink, the toys, or the pictures," I asked politely, "what's left?"

"Well," Miss Foster said, pausing as a bewildered look crossed her face, "there's the Golden Arches handle."

From the terminal, I set off on foot. My stars, but it gets hot in Memphis! In no time at all, I was sweating like a pig on a spit.

4

The atmosphere notwithstanding, here's what I like about Memphis: Whereas in some places people are rewarded for conforming to the same bland standards, in Memphis the population values eccentricity.

What others call quirky, Memphians see as artistic, or, at the very least, interesting. That's partly because southerners are suckers for a good story and a good story requires unique characters, and partly because underneath their Mississippi Delta politeness, every last one of them is as crazy as a loon and they know it.

And though I wasn't aware of it at the time, I'd soon find myself pitted against the craziest one of all.

Stormy Weather

My stepgrandmother was in the front yard watering her zinnias when I walked up.

"Land sakes!" she exclaimed, dropping the hose to the ground. "Look what the cat dragged in!"

My stepgrandmother has no cats, but she does have a dog, a retired hunting hound named Lucas, who was sleeping on the wood plank porch. Lucas raised his head, blinked his eyes, and, seeing nothing worth pursuing in the stifling summer heat, promptly returned to his nap.

"Hello, Nana," I said, submitting to a hug. "Can you put me up for a while?"

"Why, Will," she replied, "nothing would please me more."

Will.

That's what they call me. My full name is a mouthful: William Alexander Madison Lee Cooper Finn. How this happened, I don't know, but it seems to have happened to any number of southern people. I'm just happy that no one calls me Willie. My personal motto, which was given to me by my teacher in the fourth grade, is "Where there's a Will, there's a way."

By this, I think she meant that I'm resourceful.

Nana assigned me the front bedroom on the second floor, one with French doors that open to a balcony over the porch. At night, with these doors open, it's the coolest room in the house.

In the early morning, sunlight filters through the waxy leaves of the big magnolia tree, casting swaying puppet-theater silhouettes on the peeling wallpaper. From a hook on the closet door, a nightgown hung like a limp flag on a deserted Civil War battlefield.

This is a peaceful house—quite the opposite of the one I left behind.

Instead of my usual cereal poured from a box, breakfast at Nana's consisted of steaming muffins with strawberry preserves and country ham washed down with fresh-squeezed orange juice, hot coffee, and milk.

Man, I thought. *I could get used to this!*

To which fate replied, *Not so fast.*

No matter where you happen to land in life, it doesn't pay to get too comfortable. Every place is a way station to someplace else. Like ferrets cavorting in a pet store window, we're only where we are until fate takes notice of us.

"If you haven't taken a ride on a riverboat," my stepgrandmother announced, "you haven't seen Memphis."

Shortly afterward, I found myself sitting on a plank bench on the *Memphis Empress,* a statuesque white-painted stern-wheeler chugging along the Wolf River to the main channel of the wide and magnificent Mississippi.

The *Memphis Empress* is a tourist boat. Once in a while, locals rent it for special occasions, such as weddings, bar mitzvahs, and Mary Kay awards ceremonies, but most of the time the riverboat's passengers hail from India, China, Saudi Arabia, Japan, and far-off Nebraska.

Tripping across cobblestones that in a previous century served as riverboat ballast, I presented my ticket, scurried up the gangplank, and took a seat well away from the nonstop digital photography and cell phone chatter.

Had I not been intoxicated with a sense of adventure, I might have noticed the clouds rolling in from Arkansas. I have no idea what the captain's excuse may have been, but at the point at which the pilot should have turned back, the *Memphis Empress* was miles from a safe landing point, and the Mississippi River, always treacherous, had become a dark, churning, fearsome force of nature, with whirlpools, deadly flotsam, and a current so powerful, it could well have been Zeus's bathtub drain.

Wind and rain whipped us from above, while from below the river dragged us southward. At unpredictable intervals, lightning illuminated the terrified passengers, some of whom were clutching each other, their faces stricken with silent screams, while others gripped bags of Elvis souvenirs so tightly that their fingers punctured the plastic.

Without warning, the engines stopped cold. Cries went up across the deck. The *Memphis Empress,* freed from man's intervention, its huge, painted paddlewheel powered only by the storm, succumbed to the malevolent guidance of a navigator whose hometown was surely Hades. At that awful moment, every man, woman, and child on board knew in his or her heart that the *Empress* was lost, its human cargo doomed to the opaque depths of the mighty and unforgiving Father of Waters.

As it turned out, all but one of them was wrong. Gripping the slippery railing while watching the thick brown soup boil below, I was the only one thrown off when the captain, coming to his senses, suddenly restarted the engines.

"Man overboard!" I cried. Then correcting myself, I added with a sputtering *glug-glug-glug,* "Boy, actually."

But no one can hear you when the water's running.

Life on the Mississippi

Whether an event is good or bad depends on your point of view. Not just whether it's happening to you or to someone else, but whether it's rushing up to meet you or you're recalling it long after it's passed by.

They say what we fear most is the unknown.

Clearly "they" don't know much about ferrets.

I was terrified when I woke up on Ferret Island, lost, wet, and alone. But now that I've had time to think about it, I consider that day to be among the best of my life.

Except for a carefree week at church camp, I'd never been away from home. Ninety-nine percent of my life experiences had taken place within a twenty-mile radius of my house in Kansas City, and almost always in the company of adults. So once I got over the shock of discovering I was a solo castaway, and had shed a few tears over those I'd left behind, I rejoiced in my sudden liberation, although I had no idea where I was.

From where I stood in the sandy silt, my new home was an unkempt wilderness that stretched as far as the eye could see, which was maybe fifty feet before the tangled vegetation obscured everything.

A great blue heron landed on a gnarled branch of a nearby willow tree, startling me and scattering a flock of red-winged blackbirds. A bullfrog, hidden in the rushes, voiced a loud complaint.

Meanwhile, the sun, having climbed halfway up the sky, was converting the languid backwater into steam. Gnats, midges, black flies, and mosquitoes danced around my head like revelers at an all-day party. At the point at which the mucky firmament became underbrush, a snake—a water moccasin as big around as a bricklayer's arm—lay rotting in two equal pieces.

Holy smokes, I thought. *What happened to him?*

This should have been a warning to me—an omen—but I was raised amid sidewalks and shopping centers. As far as I knew, sliced snakes were simply nature's way of saying "Howdy!"

Pushing inland, I came to a clearing ringed with blackberry bushes. The grass was soft beneath my feet. Red and white clover, black-eyed Susans, Queen Anne's lace, and tiny, heart-shaped violets dotted the pocket meadow like daubs of pigment in a painting by some famous Frenchman.

Ah, I thought, failing to note the significance of the crisscross pattern of beaten grass. *I can make camp here.*

It was slow going, but using my hands, I fashioned a lean-to from willow whips—slender, limber branches torn from the trees that grew along the river. My house looked like a great upended nest. As much as it was shelter, it was also camouflage. Once inside, I was hidden from view.

Not that there *was* anyone to see me, thank goodness.

Perhaps, I admitted, *I'm not quite ready to be res - cued.*

But what would I do about supplies?

The river provided the solution.

The mighty Mississippi drains more than half the North American continent. Its tributaries stretch from within spitting distance of the Atlantic Ocean to the foothills of the towering Rockies, and through this vast network of natural plumbing flows a nonstop stream of an affluent nation's trash, a waterlogged thrift store of the unwanted, outgrown, misplaced, and swept away.

On the Mississippi River, if you keep your eyes peeled, whatever you're likely to need will eventually pass by. Conveniently, some of it will wash ashore.

Before midafternoon, after scrounging in the tangled brush, I'd retrieved a fishing pole, a frying pan, a folding chair, and a cap bearing the logo of the Kansas City Monarchs, vanished pride of the pioneering Negro Leagues. I'd also recovered a brand-new bag of barbecue-flavored potato chips and a two-liter bottle of Pepsi, both of which bobbed to the beach like jellyfish.

My life may have changed, I thought, *but my menu has not.*

Such good fortune I interpreted as a sign that fate planned nothing but easy times ahead. Of course, people see what they want to see. Our minds behave like flatterers in the court. Certainly mine chose to disregard the persistent aroma of distant skunk—or was it wet wool?—not to mention the many dried droppings from someone's poodle.

No place is perfect.

So besotted was I with my first taste of freedom that when a sharp pain suddenly registered on my ankle and a prompt inspection revealed a deep, bleeding scratch, I attributed the wound to an accidental encounter with blackberry thorns.

What an idiot I am!

Ankle bites, foul smells, sliced snakes, animal droppings, highways through the grass—come, now! How could anyone miss so many clues?

A Thief in the Night

On the island, I savored my solitude, spending the daylight hours exploring. Except for my private meadow, the interior was thick with cottonwood saplings that grew like a picket fence around the woods.

On the east side was a rocky bluff, rising at its highest point to thirty feet, providing a narrow sidewalk to the island's head, a distance of some three miles. On the western side, a beach extended to the forest. I guessed the width of the sandbar to be no more than half a mile, but crossing through the middle was next to impossible.

All in all, I assured myself, *this is a pretty nice place to be.*

I did begin to get lonely—not that I was missing anybody special. On these occasions, a nap would help. So would conversation with the local wildlife.

The heron in particular seemed to take a liking to me. He'd be at the water's edge every morning, hunting crayfish, minnows, and frogs, and he'd pause to give me a once-over before getting back to work. At sunset, he'd return to the same spot.

Sometimes, instead of fishing, he'd stand in water

up to his knees, just watching me. He was obviously an old bird, and he seemed plenty smart.

I named him Moses.

At the river's edge, I found a lot of useful stuff. I dragged a chest of drawers to my hideout, and a picnic cooler that still contained ice. I found a set of canisters, a bookshelf, a wicker wastebasket, a brass antelope, and a chipped yellow flowerpot. One morning, a brown leather Barcalounger washed up, with a library book—a murder mystery—stuck in the seat cushion. I spent the afternoon reclining in the sun and reading.

The butler's ex-wife did it.

It wasn't long before I'd salvaged so many things that I had to add an addition to my house. Using a Swiss Army knife, I cut and wove willow switches into a geodesic dome that I subdivided into three rooms with curved walls and a soaring ten-foot ceiling.

To complete the homey feeling, I stuck a mailbox out front. This, too, had washed ashore in relatively good condition, except for a few rust spots along its seams and the name FITCH in faded letters the sides.

Oh, well, I thought. *When you're the only person for miles around, Fitch is as good a name as any.*

What I did not know at the time is that *fitch* is the word for ferret fur.

One morning, while Moses was standing guard atop the tallest tree, I noticed that some of my things were missing: a deck of cards, a lighter, a calculator with a dead battery. I searched everywhere for them, but the fact is, when you live in a compact space, it doesn't take long to conduct a thorough inventory.

There was no doubt about it. Sometime during the night, my stuff had vanished.

That's odd, I thought.

A few days later, it happened again. A slotted spoon, a fishing cork, a set of keys, a rubber stamp that said Rush, and a clock without a minute hand had disappeared while I slept.

Enough's enough! I said to myself.

That night, I set a trap for the thief. On top of my chest of drawers, I placed a purple drawstring bag filled with polished pieces of colored glass—dragon's tears, they're called—opening it just enough to let a few of the faux jewels spill out.

In the moonlight, they glittered like diamonds, rubies, and emeralds—surely an irresistible temptation for the common cat burglar. My plan would have worked, too, if I hadn't dozed off sometime before midnight. When I awoke, Moses was on the river, the sun was coming up, and the dragon's tears were gone.

Dang! I thought.

The next night, I laid out my coin collection—a Vermont quarter, three dimes, a Lewis and Clark nickel, and six pennies—then stationed myself outside, behind a tree, where I could observe the entrance to my hut.

I didn't have long to wait.

Making no more noise than a shadow, a long, dark form, like a soldier inching on his belly toward enemy lines, slunk along the ground.

Frozen, I watched as it slipped inside. My heart racing, I tiptoed toward the entrance, not daring to breathe. A soft *clink-clink* sound from my bedroom told me that the thief had found the money.

I picked up a croquet mallet, its hardwood handle warped after weeks in the water. Thus armed, I approached the darkened doorway with as much confidence as one can muster when coming face-to-face with an intruder.

"You're busted, pal!" I shouted, wielding my weapon like a broadsword. "Come out with your hands up!"

Immediately, a high-pitched screech pierced the

gloom as a foul-smelling being rushed past my face like a rifle shot, nicking my ear.

I'm hit! I thought, dropping the mallet and falling to the hard dirt floor.

Into the Woods

His masked eyes glowed like smoldering coals. His ears lay flat against his head. His sharp teeth glistened, his whiskers twitched, and a sneer crossed his ratlike face.

It was the largest creature of its kind I've ever seen: a ferret as big as a Florida alligator.

Holy smokes! I thought, as the mutant weasel turned and crashed toward the woods. *This is like sighting Bigfoot, or the Loch Ness Monster, or King Kong!*

Nature has endowed man with two equal but opposite impulses. On the one hand, there's fear, an instinct that keeps us from getting killed before our time. On the other hand, however, is an equally strong impulse called curiosity, that sirenlike attraction to mystery that's responsible for the untimely deaths of a million cats, as well as the accumulated knowledge of mankind.

Should I follow the ferret? I pondered.

Although I'd occasionally stopped to watch these domesticated polecats dozing in their hammocks in the pet store, the ferret facts at my fingertips were few.

One thing I knew is that they're carnivorous—they eat meat, and they enjoy it freshly killed. In this respect they're indistinguishable from saber-toothed tigers, great white sharks, and grizzly bears.

Normally, they feed on rats, or rabbits, or chickens, but a giant ferret, I reasoned, is bound to go for bigger prey. If a two-pound ferret can take down a five-pound rabbit on the run, imagine what a fifty-pounder can do to one small city boy.

If my calculator hadn't been both inoperative and stolen, I would have done the math.

As it was, I simply shuddered.

I'm no daredevil, but the strong scent of ferret pee convinced me that I could track this monster from a safe distance.

Perhaps if I locate his lair, I reasoned, *I can turn the tables on him and recover my stuff while he's out.*

But that's not all that crossed my mind that night. That gigantic, thieving weasel was an incredible discovery. If I could study him, take his picture, or, even better, bring him back alive, I could publish my findings in *Scientific American*!

A wild giant ferret?

Heck, I'd just gotten a glimpse of a Nobel Prize!

With only the stink and the stars to guide me, I struck out through the wilderness.

In medieval Europe, the forests were the dwelling places of outlaws, black magic, hungry wolves, and demons. Dark and mysterious, they were places children were forbidden to enter. Fairy tales, those terrifying narratives of talking carnivores, deceitful goblins, and evil witches, were created to warn kids about the dangers of straying from home. Although spun from the ignorance and imagination of adults, the stories contained grim kernels of truth. Bad things happen in the wild: Children disappear—or worse.

But what were my choices? To hide in my willow hut forever?

No! I told myself. *I must seize the day*—carpe diem—*or in this case, the night!*

If only I'd gone back to bed.

Weeds as tall as fence posts brushed against my

body. Branches slapped my unwashed face. Vines, knotted and curled like serpents, snatched at my ankles, pulling me away from my goal.

Despite these distractions, I pressed on.

The pungent trail of ferret pee took me deeper into the forest. From time to time I paused to listen, but when you're born and bred in the suburbs, one rustling sound seems much like another.

I sniffed the ground, the air, the trees, changing direction whenever the smell grew faint. On and on into the aromatic shadows I went, farther and farther from the safety of my willow hut, until the inevitable at last occurred:

I got lost.

Compared to Kansas City, Ferret Island is not a big place. But Kansas City has streets with names and numbers and lights, and signs marking every corner.

There are no signs in the woods.

Heck, there are no corners!

There's just the deep, anonymous dark.

Hmmm, I thought. *Maybe this wasn't such a good idea.*

Under the circumstances, the only thing to do was climb a tree and wait for dawn.

As with so many small decisions, this one turned

out to have momentous consequences. Within a few minutes after I'd settled in, resting sidesaddle on a peeling paper-bark limb halfway up a river birch, I heard a gruff, disgruntled voice—a man's voice—speak the following words:

"Ding-dang it all to Singapore! Now where'd I put my glasses this time!"

Attack of the Giant Ferret

The first thing that came to mind was pirates. Cutthroats. Robbers. River gangsters, murderers, cold-blooded thieves.

But then, I asked myself, *do pirates wear glasses?*

An eye patch, certainly. It's as much a part of the uniform as a talking parrot. But glasses? It seemed unlikely. But if not a high seas terrorist, then what? Had I stumbled on the hidden home of a hermit?

Well, I thought, *we're practically neighbors. Maybe I should introduce myself.*

But no sooner did I think this than I rejected the notion.

Hermits, I reasoned, *are hermits for a very good reason.*

Leaves like angel wings fluttered softly, invisible in the night breeze. Songbirds, nesting restlessly, cried out in their dreams. Nocturnal rodents, having no time to lose, bustled through the brush below, while in the distance, somewhere between me and the state of Mississippi, chugging tugs nudged a barge train up the river. And the hermit—if that's what he was—said not another word.

Did I really hear what I thought I heard? I wondered.

At first light, I dropped to the forest floor, following a narrow path that wound through the trees. Although perfumed with more than a hint of rot, in the dappled shade of the woodland, the morning air was cool. This was fortunate, for the path was unusually convoluted, with more bends and twists and cul-de-sacs than normal travel requires. It was as if the trail had been blazed by moonstruck rabbits.

But even with such a cockeyed roadway, on a tiny Mississippi River island, it's not long before you get to where you're going. Turning a corner, I found myself at a clearing, where I stared in disbelief at the storybook illustration before me.

At first glance, it looked like a scene from Walt Disney's *Snow White,* with sunbeams illuminating a gingerbread cottage and bunnies sniffing blossoms near the door.

But a closer look told a different story. This house wasn't sponge cake and sugarplums; it was made from empty bottles—beer bottles, wine bottles, liquor bottles—even an olive jar or two—stacked on their sides and cemented together in crooked rows like my Uncle Festus's teeth.

In the streaming shafts of sunlight, the structure gave off the glow of an alien spacecraft. And that's not the half of it. The critters cavorting near the doorway weren't rabbits at all—they were ferrets, seven of them, each bigger than a bird dog and all of them looking in my direction.

Uh-oh, I thought. *Now what do I do?*

Arching his back, the smallest of the group, a young male weighing perhaps thirty-five pounds, danced sideways on his tiptoes, baring his teeth.

"Easy, boy," I said.

Continuing his zigzagging advance, he made an ominous chirping sound deep inside his throat.

"*Chi-chi-chi!*" he said.

As mutant ferrets go, this was a fine example. His soft outer fur was a pattern of chocolate brown stripes, and when he moved, a creamy white underfur was revealed. The effect of this peekaboo coloration was a pearlescent appearance, like a rainbow trout glistening in a mountain stream.

So captivating was he that I would have continued to admire him had he not suddenly opened his mouth wide and leapt through the air, landing at my feet.

At such close quarters, toe-to-toe and nose-to-fur, you learn that a ferret's smell is not a rancid stink like the monkey house at the zoo, but a rich and complex bouquet on the order of Ethiopian coffee, Honduran cigars, or Parmesano Reggiano cheese, an aroma that's immediately identifiable, a musky essence that announces, "I am weasel, smell me more."

You also find out that ferrets have claws as sharp as those of any jungle cat, five on each padded, furry foot—twenty stiletto-like weapons in all. Add to this a mouthful of razor-sharp teeth, and it's no wonder that a ferret can instantly dispatch an adversary many times its size.

Had this been the only threat, my chances for survival would have been slim to none, but this guy had friends, two of which seemed interested in participating in the pending massacre.

If I'd had any spit left in me, I would have gulped.

Without further warning, the first ferret attacked my feet, twitching his tail as he shook his head from side to side like a Jack Russell terrier snapping the neck of a Norway rat. Then, inexplicably, he bounded away with a chickenlike chuckle, his iridescent body alternately arching and extending like an inchworm on a leaf.

Shaking with fear, I looked down, expecting to see a widening pool of my own blood. Instead, I discovered that the tricky little demon had tied my shoelaces together!

So that's your game! I thought, falling flat on my face into a patch of wild onions.

A World-Famous Neighbor

"Mr. Fitch, I presume," said the voice above my head. "How nice of you to drop in, so to speak."

The orator was, I concluded, the hermit, who, on helping me to my feet, turned out to be a stocky, rumpled man well into his middle years.

He'd obviously located his glasses—bent silver-framed bifocals—and he wore them askew, balanced on a large, bulbous nose.

To my horror, I realized why his glasses didn't fit: He was missing his left ear! Where that handy paired appendage should have been was only an opening, a bellybutton on the side of his head.

How on earth? I wondered, gaping.

The hermit responded with a drawn-out frown, during which I noted that his complexion was ruddy, his eyebrows bushy, and his hair gray at the temples, while on the top of his head he sported a baseball cap celebrating the famed Kansas City Monarchs.

"I think that may be my hat," I said.

"I doubt it," he replied.

"Also, my name isn't Fitch," I added. "It's Finn. Will Finn."

"I see," he answered. "And mine's Daschell Potts, but if you ever tell anyone, I'll sic Jaws here on you."

With this threat, a monster ferret with black and white fur opened a tooth-filled mouth.

"My lips are sealed," I quickly agreed.

"In that case," Mr. Potts said, "please join me for breakfast."

Sunlight causes a bottle house to glow like a cathedral. Light bends, twists, radiates, and diffuses, creating a dazzling, mesmerizing effect. Entering the house of Mr. Potts was like crossing into another dimension.

"Are you any relation to the author?" I asked. "The one who wrote *Folderol*?"

"If only I could put that behind me," he replied with a pained expression.

"But *Folderol* is a modern classic!" I cried. "Everybody says so."

"That's the problem," Mr. Potts replied. "If *Folderol* is such a high-water mark, what's the point of publishing anything else? So I quit."

"You quit writing?" I responded. "That's terrible!"

"I quit publishing," Mr. Potts clarified. "My daily scribbles continue to amuse me."

Turning his back, Mr. Potts placed two fish fillets into a skillet. While these were frying, he reached into a bag and retrieved some paper-wrapped cheeseburgers that he tossed to the ferrets. Ketchup dripped across the floor.

Hmmm, I thought. *Where'd he get those?*

"Anyway," Mr. Potts continued, "I prefer the anonymous life. Among other things, you don't have the expense of dry cleaning."

I knew that more than most people, hermits value their private time. So I didn't take offense when my host announced, "Nice meeting you, Finn. You can show yourself out."

I took a few wrong turns but eventually found my way back to the willow hut, where Moses was pacing the roof as if he'd been worried about me.

By now the temperature had risen to nearly a hundred degrees—too hot to do anything. I lay on my back in my living room and thought about the last twenty-four hours.

All things considered, I liked my new life. First and foremost, I enjoyed my freedom. But when you live alone, it's important to know your neighbors, and, as neighbors go, mine was extraordinary.

Daschell Potts was an authentic legend. Following the publication of *Folderol,* a lot of very smart people said literature would never again be the same.

In the unlikely event you haven't read it, *Folderol* is ostensibly written for kids, but it is in fact an allegory for us all. With deft, poetic phrasing, the author recounts the journey of a duckling circling a pond, an innocent adrift on unknown waters, who eventually returns, sadder but wiser, to the point where his journey began.

I first read *Folderol* in fourth grade, and it changed my life. Now I was sharing an island with its creator.

Go figure! I thought.

As the sun sent sweat streaming down my face, my thoughts shifted from bringing giant ferrets to the attention of science (and a jaded world primed for new amusements) to getting my hands on whatever Mr. Potts had been writing since he left the book scene. If I could deliver this literary landmark to the right people, it would be the publishing event of the century!

Is this wrong? I asked myself.

Only technically, I answered.

The more enlightened way of seeing it was that I'd be doing civilization a tremendous favor, providing a peek at what our greatest living writer had been thinking all these years.

Why, the man's a national treasure! I rationalized. *For him to keep his thoughts to himself—well, that's the real crime.*

This illustrates one of the chief hazards of living alone. In a conversation with another person, you'd notice if your listener rolled his or her eyes, or looked away, disgusted and appalled. But when you're talking to yourself, all you get is agreement, no matter how wacko—or how dangerous—your plan.

Words of Warning

There's a scene in *Folderol* in which the duckling—lost, lonely, and exhausted from his circuitous paddling quest—finds a note inside a bottle. Unable to read, the naïve protagonist, assuming that what he's discovered is edible, swallows the crumpled paper whole. Alas, only the reader realizes that the note is a discount certificate for Peking duck at the nearby Golden Panda Chinese Buffet.

With this brilliant metaphor, Daschell Potts reminds us how we spend our days oblivious to life's many dangers. Nobody knows what lies ahead, he tells us, but eventually what comes next will be the end of the line.

Like Mr. Potts's delusional duckling, I proceeded down my self-directed path ignorant of the consequences. Get the manuscript, get off the island, get it to those half a dozen New Yorkers who, when not having lunch, control all publishing—in my mind, it was as simple as one, two, three, with three being the toughest part.

And then the first storm hit.

What I learned later is that it was the collapsing edge of the now infamous Hurricane Bud, the storm that battered New Orleans for two days before moving inland to wreak havoc on Jackson, Vicksburg, and Tallulah. Heavy rains, tornadoes, and widespread flooding followed in Bud's wake.

The lower Mississippi was an inland sea, while a treacherous backwash swirled as far north as Ferret Island, lapping like a pack of thirsty weasels at the shore.

My willow hut, tightly woven and anchored to the trees with strips of braided green bark, defied the fury of the storm. Under the circumstances, even Moses concluded that my house was the best chance for survival. Swallowing his pride, the stately heron took up residence in my living room.

A frightened ferret showed up, too—a stranger—a gray-striped polecat weighing nearly twenty pounds. He had a friendly face, sad eyes, stubby bowed legs, a long tail, and a noticeable tummy, and as the thunder exploded outside, he curled up on the Barcalounger and went to sleep.

I named him Jim.

How quickly we act to fill the empty spaces in our lives! One minute I am living alone. The next, I'm the breadwinner for a blended family of three. It wasn't an ideal arrangement, of course. I would have preferred a natural brother, or a sister, or a girlfriend, but in this life, you play the hand you're dealt.

As the storm raged on, I cleaned my house, tended to my visitors, and boiled a pot of pungent crayfish stew.

What else could I do?

I suppose I could've thought about certain people back in Kansas City and felt sorry for causing them to worry—if that's what they were doing—but, frankly, I hadn't gotten over being angry. Besides, I had a new life now, with a noble mission and potentially interesting friends.

Considering their differences in species, Jim and Moses got along surprisingly well, sharing a food dish and improvising a competition with a tennis ball. When the rain stopped I figured they'd dash right out the door, but Moses poked his beak outside, clicked a signal to Jim, and the two of them went back to their game.

That's when I recalled the scene in *Folderol* where

the duckling, thinking that because the rain has stopped the danger has passed, paddles from the protective boughs of a weeping willow tree and is struck by lightning.

Miraculously, the duckling isn't killed, but his downy feathers are singed like blackened Cajun catfish, his beak is bleached a whalebone white, and whatever thoughts remain are scrambled by an intercepted cell phone signal playing Pachelbel's Canon in D over and over again.

In all of contemporary literature, I thought, *nobody makes a point like Daschell Potts!*

Since I couldn't shake the man's hand, I shook my head in amazement instead.

When the storm resumed with its second wind, and the rain beat down even harder than before, I marveled at the proof that my new neighbor was a fount of wisdom, a gifted genius, a worthy cultural icon. Clearly, it was my responsibility to find his manuscript and bring it to the attention of a desperate world.

I imagined newspaper headlines, interviews on TV, and my face on the cover of *Time* magazine: WILL FINN, THE BOY WHO RESCUED WISDOM.

Outside the hut, the storm raged on, while inside

my head thoughts flitted from one grandiose scene to another, like ruby-throated hummingbirds flaunting their colors in Nana's Memphis garden.

Suddenly, my reverie was interrupted.

Where were Moses and Jim? I hadn't seen them for a while, and inside the hut everything was quiet.

Too quiet.

Oh, no! I thought. *I've left a twenty-pound poultry-loving carnivore with an elderly five-pound stork.*

Oops.

Down in the Valley

"Moses," I called out in panic. "Are you okay?"

But the only answer was the howling of the wind.

Rushing to the living room, I found Jim alone, his beady eyes glistening, his tail twitching like a cat's. On the floor were two gray feathers. A third feather was in Jim's mouth.

"Dang!" I shouted. "Dang, dang, dang, dang, dang!"

Looking at me as if I were a Martian, Jim arched his furry back, danced sideways across the floor, made a low *chi-chi-chi* sound, and bit my toe. But before I could manage to shout "Ow," the missing Moses

35

moseyed in, his silence explained by the tennis ball stuck firmly on his pointy beak.

As Daschell Potts so memorably observed in *Folderol,* "Unless you're a flea within a few feet of a passing dog, jumping to conclusions never pays off."

The Mississippi River is one of the great natural wonders of the world. This vast, deceptively sluggish waterway exerts more power than a million train engines front to back on a downhill curve. It's this compelling fact that made swimming from the island inadvisable.

So what am I going to do once I nab Mr. Potts's pre-cious pages? I asked myself.

Obviously I'd need a boat.

Or a raft.

Materials for a raft seemed easy to come by. The island had plenty of trees, and what wood I couldn't cut I could harvest from the beach. What I lacked was know-how. But with the smartest man in America— possibly the world—living only a short walk away, this obstacle, too, could be overcome if I was clever enough.

If? I thought to myself. *Why, if I hadn't been given so many names already, "Clever" would most cer-tainly have been the middle one.*

Bursting with self-confidence, I set out to pay a return visit to my neighbor.

"I'll see you guys later," I said to Moses and Jim. "I have an appointment with destiny."

It's a good thing destiny hadn't confirmed the meeting time, because I would have been late. Everything takes longer than you think—even a stroll through the woods.

The storm had washed out the path and backflow had turned the forest floor into a desolate swamp, with chest-deep chocolate water, clouds of blood-thirsty insects, and squirming nests of poisonous snakes.

My only choice was to take the long way around, along the bluffs, then double back through a section of the island I hadn't yet explored.

No problem, I thought. *There's plenty of daylight, and not a lot of island.*

Crows as big as macaws shouted encouragement from the treetops as I marched along, whistling a tune from my childhood. Grasshoppers, crickets, locusts, and cicadas accompanied me with a thousand-creature rhythm band. The last fleeting remnants of Hurricane Bud—wispy clouds high in the sky—drifted like dryer lint on any given weekday in the Kansas City suburbs.

It's good to be alive, I thought.

An hour into my journey, I sat on a rock, opened my knapsack, and prepared to treat myself to the cheese and crackers I'd recovered a couple of days before when a fisherman's lunch box washed ashore.

But the moment I tasted the cheese, I was struck by a strong, unpleasant odor. My immediate reaction was that the cheese had gone bad, but then it dawned on me that I knew this scent. It was the unmistakable aroma of wet weasel, the sharp, sour smell of stinkmarten, that sickly sweet stench of overripe chrysanthemums that comes from leaving your ferrets out in the rain.

It was quite strong and very fresh.

A lizard skittered away when I stood up to investigate. Butterflies scattered with each successive step. Ascending a slight rise on which a fairy ring of mushrooms grew, I found myself at the lip of a ravine.

The scene that greeted me took my breath away.

Far below, the valley swarmed with oversize ferrets—a hundred or more of them—bounding, tumbling, gamboling in the summer sun. Some had babies at their sides. Some were feeding. Others languished in the shade.

It was a vast, furry city of weasels—brown, black, and shoe-leather tan—long, sharp-nosed, black-masked weasels, pulsating like fishing worms in a rusty Folgers can.

But this was not the most astonishing sight. That distinction was reserved for an activity at the edge of the teeming pageant, where, like a blazing comet in a clear night sky, one animal stood out above the rest: a snow white, red-eyed, gray-whiskered albino giant, a ferret as big as a Sears Craftsman lawn tractor, eating what appeared to be a McDonald's Quarter-Pounder from a one-eared man's outstretched hand.

Holy cow! I thought.

The Scene of the Crime

As if he sensed he was being observed, the white ferret looked in my direction, his ruby-colored eyes glowing like lasers aimed right at me. Immediately, I ducked beneath an outcropping and lay still.

Luckily for me, ferrets have poor eyesight, and with

those elongated bodies and short, stumpy legs, they can't run fast through open country, either, expending as much energy skipping sideways as they do moving forward.

Where ferret propulsion reigns supreme is underground, through rabbit holes, gopher tunnels, and prairie dog towns. You wouldn't want to try to outrun a ferret inside a sewer pipe. You'd never make it.

Suddenly, it dawned on me that Mr. Potts was fully occupied.

Now's the perfect time to get the manuscript, I told myself.

After a brief bivouac in the rocks, I inched around the noisy weasel encampment, arriving at Mr. Potts's bottle house before sundown.

Conveniently, the door was wide open.

A writer's desk tells a story, frequently as well as the writer himself. Where it's positioned, what it's made of, the knickknacks that adorn its edges—all of these provide glimpses into the writer's soul.

Hewn from rugged oak, Mr. Potts's desk read like a case history in modern psychological archaeology.

On its thick slab surface the author had positioned a typewriter, a kerosene lamp, a pencil jar, a brass ashtray, four butane lighters, reading glasses with a single temple, a wicker basket filled with seashells, a white wildflower in a bud vase, a faded Flintstones jelly glass, a yellow plastic duck, stacks of books, paper, notepads, and index cards, and three quarts of Canadian whiskey, one of which was mostly consumed.

I stand in the presence of genius, I thought reverently.

But there was no time to lose. The mission took precedence over the moment.

The center drawer of Mr. Potts's desk had two matching black iron circles dangling on either side of an ironclad keyhole.

I tugged at one of the rings.

The drawer didn't budge.

Once again I pulled, this time harder. Stubbornly, it still refused to open.

Why would you leave your door open but lock your desk drawer? I wondered.

Frustrated, I grabbed both handles and gave a hearty yank.

With a sound like untrimmed fingernails screeching across a chalkboard, the drawer slid open about six inches, revealing a thick, tattered manuscript bound with two fat rubber bands.

Aha! I thought. *Success is mine!*

But barely a heartbeat later, just as I was hoping to examine what no human eyes had seen before, save those of the author himself, an echo of the screeching drawer cried back at me from the woods.

But it was no echo, of course.

It was the battle cry of the giant ferret.

Mr. Potts had returned.

In a single deft movement, I jumped up from his chair and blocked the open drawer with my body, just as the legendary recluse strode like a returning Odysseus into the room.

"Hello," I said, gasping. "How's it going?"

"Perhaps you should tell me," he replied gruffly.

"Say, I don't mean to be rude," I jabbered on, "but I couldn't help but notice your left ear. If you don't mind my asking, what happened?"

"What's that?" he answered, cupping his good ear with his hand.

"Your ear," I repeated, pointing to my own.

"Oh," he muttered, nodding. "Polecat got it. That one out there."

He gestured through the door to where a dozen

giant ferrets were roaming around looking for something to do—or worse.

"Took it off in a single chomp," he continued. "Hurt something awful."

"Golly," I responded. "That's terrible."

"Yes, it is," Mr. Potts agreed. "Some creatures aren't as trustworthy as they might first appear."

With this comment, he removed his lopsided spectacles and stared me square in the eye.

Without his glasses, Mr. Potts looked a lot like a lizard—a chameleon, an iguana, or possibly a Gila monster—with circles within circles of loose leathery skin surrounding hard, marble eyes.

Involuntarily, I shivered.

"Sun's setting," he observed. "It's going to be cool tonight."

For his sake, I wish I could report that those eyes missed nothing as he surveyed the luminescent shapes in the natural twilight of his home, but this was not the case. Mr. Potts failed to notice my hand slowly reach behind me and close his desk drawer.

In addition to his obvious hearing problem, the old yarn spinner was as nearsighted as the smelly members of his bizarre menagerie.

Whew! I thought. *Close call!*

A Case of Mistaken Identity

Clearly, since he'd first burst onto the literary scene like a bottle rocket, the years had not treated Mr. Potts kindly. Neither, given the grim explanation for his missing ear, had his ferrets. If they weren't murderers already, they'd surely had a taste of human blood.

"Tell me, Mr. Finn," Mr. Potts inquired, "what are you hoping to accomplish?"

"Me?" I replied nervously. "You mean, when I grow up?"

"Let's start with right now," Mr. Potts clarified.

"Well," I answered, glancing guiltily at the desk drawer in which his manuscript lay unread. "I'd really like to learn how to build a raft."

"A reasonable goal," Mr. Potts observed.

"Do you know anything about river rafts?" I asked.

Mr. Potts paused in thought.

Suddenly, a strange smile passed across his weather-beaten face, like on a snake when it first spies a baby bird fluttering helplessly in a bush.

"As a matter of fact," he hissed, "I do."

The lecture that ensued was fascinating and rich in detail, especially the part about using green wood and interlocking slipknots, secrets of raft construction I never would have guessed.

The only problem was that though I'd located the priceless Potts manuscript, I hadn't actually gotten it—not yet.

But I had managed to get the great man to practically build me a getaway vehicle with his own two hands.

Ha! I thought in self-congratulation. *He may be the smartest guy around, but I sure outfoxed him this time. That was like shooting fish in a barrel.*

Not surprisingly, my pride was to prove premature. If only I'd remembered these prescient words from Mr. Potts's prizewinning novel, *Folderol:*

"Fish rarely are found in barrels," the author sagely observed, "and discharging a firearm into one invariably renders it useless."

Another obstacle also emerged: Because my island neighbor had talked so long, I found myself stumbling home in the dark.

Oh, well, I thought. *I've done this before.*

Once I was inside the swampy woods, the night became as black as night can be. The moon, when visible, was but a sliver in the sky, the stars mere perforations.

Stopping, I rubbed my eyes, hoping to improve my vision. Everything looked different. Nothing was distinct. All I could make out were shifting shapes with no edges—a foreign phantom world.

Who in his right mind ventures out in the night - time? I asked myself.

Only furtive, sneaky creatures—such as killer ferrets—that conduct their shady business while the more noble animals, the ones whose consciences are clear, are asleep.

Of course, I was up, traipsing about like a fool.

Hmmm, I thought, my body shaking involuntarily.

Not that I was scared.

From out of the shadows a fat toad hopped across my foot.

"Yikes!" I cried.

"Awk!" came a sharp reply.

Ahead, alighting on a sassafras tree, the great blue heron Moses appeared as a black silhouette against a ghost gray sky, at that moment a welcome, comforting sight.

Interestingly, in his stiletto-shaped beak my loyal guide carried a magazine—more Mississippi River bounty—that, on our arrival home, turned out to be a soggy but salvageable recent edition of the Sunday newspaper supplement *Parade*. With Moses standing sentinel outside, and Jim dozing by my bedside, I separated its sticky pages by candlelight.

A section on entertainment personalities caught my eye, consisting primarily of questions from readers asking, "Whatever happened to So-and-So?"

Former child star Julia Tufts ("Becky" from *Hannigan's Island*), I learned, was now captain of her high school swim team in Marmaduke, Arkansas; disgraced former Louisiana congressman Pierre "Hercules" Narf was throwing pottery in a minimum-security prison in nearby Forrest City, Arkansas; and novelist Daschell Potts, the acclaimed, enigmatic author of *Folderol,* I read, my mouth falling open in shock, had been killed by a band of Canadian fossil poachers while exploring the wilds of western Kansas, although, sadly, his body was never found.

"Holy smokes!" I cried aloud. "Can this be so?"

My outburst brought the ever-vigilant Moses flapping noisily into the room while sending Jim scurrying to his hideout beneath the bed.

"It's okay, fellows," I said.

But, of course, it wasn't.

I had no reason to doubt the veracity of *Parade*. If

something is published in black and white in your Sunday paper, it's undoubtedly true. Everybody knows that.

But since that's the case, then who was the one-eared hermit holding court with weasels at the bottle house in the woods?

Venus Rising

I'm not sure how long I'd been settled in on Ferret Island before it struck me that I'd been living in a boys' club. Me. Moses. Jim. The strange person calling himself Daschell Potts.

It was as if there were a sign posted on the beach:

No Girls Allowed

I do recall when the insight occurred, however. I was coming home from cutting down a honey locust tree late one afternoon and found Moses with another heron, a bird taller and thinner than himself—and considerably noisier. The newcomer was squawking, flapping its wings, stomping its storklike foot, and pecking at Moses's face.

Poor guy, I thought.

Incredibly, Moses stood there taking it, as if he was resigned to such hysterical henpecking. That's what made me think the new arrival must be his wife.

Seeing me staring at them, Moses cringed and turned his head away, as sheepish as a waterfowl can be.

"That's okay," I said with a chuckle. "You can introduce us later."

But as I now know, one must be wary about finding amusement in the misfortunes of others. Such a response triggers a phenomenon known as the Law of the Twin Banana Peels. If you laugh at a person slipping on a banana peel on the sidewalk, within minutes another banana peel will appear, but this time you will be the victim of the pratfall.

Beware.

What Moses was coping with was nothing compared to what fate had in store for me. No sooner had I returned to the sanctity of my willow hut than I was face-to-face with a stranger, a girl, dripping wet, dressed in a bathrobe—mine—and combing out her hair.

"Oh, hello," she said. "I hope you don't mind. The door was open."

"There isn't a door," I replied.

"Well, then," she said, "that proves it."

She seemed to be about my age, maybe a little older. With her hair so wet, it was hard to tell, but her face was cute and, for some reason, familiar.

"Have we met before?" I asked.

"I don't see how that's possible," she replied. "I just got here." Then she added with obvious annoyance, "But you really should get a door. I just chased a rat out of here that was as big as a vacuum cleaner."

Jim! I thought.

An awkward silence passed between us as she looked around the room.

"My name's Will," I said, offering my hand.

"If you say so," she responded, continuing to comb the tangles from her hair.

Her nose, I noticed, wiggled like a rabbit's when she frowned.

"Do you have a name?" I asked.

The girl sighed and cinched up my robe.

"Julia," she confessed. "But I already have a boyfriend, if that's where you're headed. He's coming to rescue me as soon as they notice that I'm missing."

"Who's 'they'?" I asked.

"My swim team," she replied. "We were on a

steamboat cruise from Memphis. I accidentally slipped off the railing."

"I think that must happen a lot," I observed. "It makes you wonder why they don't put up a fence."

"They certainly need to do something," Julia agreed.

As the sun set over Arkansas, the sky bled crimson, pink, and purple in soft, alternating streaks, like a watercolor masterwork in a London museum. Red-tailed hawks rushed to distant nesting sites, and bats, thousands of skittering black dots, poured out from caves. A fat orange moon loomed above the treetops, and stars appeared, sprinkled across the heavens like pixie dust.

"I wonder what's keeping him," Julia said.

"Maybe he got lost," I suggested.

Julia grimaced.

"Since it seems you're going to be here for a while," I suggested, "maybe I should let you in on this island's secret. But brace yourself, because unless you've seen it with your own eyes, what I'm about to reveal may be hard to believe."

"Whatever," she replied.

"There's a one-eared hermit living nearby who trains packs of wild ferrets—giant ones, with teeth as long as Ginsu knives," I announced. "And that's not the most amazing part. Guess who he claims he is? None other than the great Daschell Potts!"

"Who?" Julia said.

"Daschell Potts," I repeated. "The writer."

"Never heard of him," Julia said, not bothering to stifle a yawn. "Goodness, it's getting late."

"But . . ." I started to say.

Julia stood up and stretched her arms.

"About the sleeping arrangements," she said.

"Oh, well, I was thinking . . ." I began.

"It's a clear night," Julia interrupted. "Why don't you sleep outside?"

Jim was cowering in a pile of leaves, where I settled down to join him.

It wasn't that uncomfortable.

Just a handful of spiders, a centipede, a few black beetles, and a couple of ticks.

A Bend in the River

Rising early, I washed up at the river, checked the overnight flotsam delivery, and fished for catfish while Jim poked around in yellow sneezeweed.

The air was pleasantly warm, with a westerly breeze perfumed with a hint of diesel fuel, a reminder that the Mississippi River is a thriving place of business.

Suddenly, I was eager to join in.

Today, I told myself, *I'm going to build a raft. And after that, I'll change the world.*

Assuming, of course, that the hermit was indeed Daschell Potts, which could be determined by reading the manuscript.

You can't fake genius.

"Where've you been?" Julia demanded. "I can't find anything in this so-called house. Where do you keep your toaster?"

"Toaster?" I repeated. "Whatever for? We're having fish."

"Again?" Julia complained.

From the trees came raucous squawking—Moses's wife.

"Listen, Julia," I said. "Fish is good for you. But if you really want something else, I'll see what I can do."

"Aren't you sweet," she cooed, placing her hand on my forearm. "Do you think we could have waffles?"

Her touch sent lightning bolts up my arm.

"How many would you like?" I replied.

Later, after a meal of hand-indented, homemade nut flour griddlecakes with wild honey, Julia pronounced the meal a success.

"Mmmm," she said, licking her fingers. "You know what would be good tonight? Lasagna. I love lasagna with meat sauce."

"Actually," I explained, dabbing mud on my bee stings, "I was hoping to make do with leftovers. I've got to build a raft."

"Oh?" she said. "Will it take long?"

Although loneliness sometimes can be a problem, there's a lot to be said for living by yourself. You can set your own hours, think your own thoughts, and make any odor you're capable of. When another person enters the picture, everything changes.

"Why don't you wear socks?" Julia asked.

"I don't have any," I replied.

"You should get some," she decreed.

And so on.

By the end of the day, I'd failed to cut down a single tree. While Julia enjoyed mushroom and berry salad, the raft remained landlocked inside my head.

Tomorrow, I told myself, *I'll build the raft, get the manuscript, and be on my way to a place in history.*

But, of course, once again I was wrong.

The day began with a list of things Julia required—bathtub, toothbrush, hand mirror—before I knew it, it was nightfall and I still had no raft.

Day after day, the pattern repeated itself. I'd awake raring to go, eager to carry out my plan for the unknown work of the world's greatest writer, only to be thwarted by the demands of my uninvited houseguest. Julia wanted to take a walk. Julia wanted crayfish gumbo. Julia wanted gardenias planted by the hut. Julia. Julia. Julia.

"Listen," I said one balmy evening. "I've been thinking. What if I occasionally take a day off to do something by myself?"

"Like what?" she asked. "Bowling? Poker? *Monday Night Football?*"

"Of course not," I answered. "Just something that doesn't involve so much, you know, togetherness."

Without speaking, she stormed into the hut, then barricaded the entrance with my Barcalounger.

"I think that went okay," I said to Jim. "At least I managed to introduce the subject."

"*Chi-chi-chi,*" Jim replied.

At sunset, I came across Moses fishing among the cattails. A flock of geese passed overhead, forming a long, looping letter *Y*. Gazing up at the travelers,

Moses stretched out his little-used wings. From the shadows came the squawk of the other heron. Immediately, he put his head down and went back to fishing.

How did this happen? I wondered. *How did we go from being as free as a bird to as captive as a canary?*

The next morning, after breakfast, I announced, "I'm going to see Mr. Potts."

"Suit yourself," Julia answered. "Just don't forget, you have responsibilities at home."

Home? I thought.

The man who might be Daschell Potts was at his desk, typing. On the floor were three giant ferrets tussling like young tigers.

Entering the room, I felt as if I were interrupting Einstein with a half-completed equation on his blackboard.

"Mr. Potts?" I said.

The author spun around, jerked the paper from his typewriter, and slipped it into the desk drawer. In those few seconds, I caught a glimpse of the sentence "We attack at dawn."

Aha! I thought. *There's no doubt about his identity now. Only the great Daschell Potts could craft a phrase like that.*

But what, I wondered, *does it mean?*

A Change of Venue

We attack at dawn.

Daschell Potts's magnum opus was an adventure novel!

Suddenly, inspiration struck, a way to kill two birds with one stone, if a person is so inclined: how to improve my troubled life with Julia and get the Potts manuscript, as well.

"Mr. Potts?" I said. "May I ask you a question?"

"Speak into my good ear," he replied, pointing to the only one he had.

"Why do you live like this?" I asked.

"Ah," he answered, his face relaxing into a half smile. "Inside each of us is a calling to the water's edge. Some pay vast fortunes to live in sprawling mansions by the sea. Others crowd into tiny hand-hewn cabins within sight of distant lakes. And some, like myself, gather in the wilderness by the rushing river. There is a voice within water that speaks directly to our souls, saying, 'Here, mankind, here is where you belong.'"

Ask a writer a simple question!

"Okay, sure," I said, "but what I'm driving at is why you live by yourself. I need a place to stay. My roommate is impossible."

"Hmmm," he said. "Maybe for a couple of days."

That afternoon, I packed my belongings.

"Well," I told Julia. "See you later."

"Sure," she replied. "No hard feelings."

"Okay, then," I added. "Goodbye."

"Have a nice time," Julia said.

With mixed emotions, I turned my back on the willow hut and headed toward the woods. In a tulip tree at the edge of the clearing, monarch butterflies, en route to an equatorial retreat, rested in the branches, each one folded in half, like little orange origami hands in prayer.

"Will, wait, don't go!" a voice cried out.

I turned to see an angel haloed in the doorway of the hut. My heart leapt up when I beheld Julia begging me to stay.

But why, I wondered, *is she waving a broom?*

"Wait up, Will!" she called again.

Swinging the broom above her head, Julia launched a swat to Jim's narrow rump that sent the ferret tumbling like a croquet ball through the grass.

"You forgot your weasel!" Julia cried.

In *Folderol,* Daschell Potts's masterstroke, the duckling, in his journey around the pond, wakes each morning not only not knowing where he is, but thinking, as he shakes off the fog of sleep, that he's where he was the day before.

In other words, the author seems to be saying, in that incisive way that's uniquely his, that the relentless forward motion of life keeps us permanently confused.

Certainly I was when I awoke the next morning expecting to be in (or near) my willow hut.

Huh? I thought, turning over on an unfamiliar canvas cot.

Lying on my back, I watched as dawn struck the walls of Mr. Potts's bottle house, setting everything aglow—Mr. Potts's desk, his table, the giant ferrets sleeping on the floor. Interestingly, as I identified each luminous object in the room, there was no sign of Mr. Potts himself.

Well, I'll be, I thought. *Now's my chance!*

Stumbling to my feet, I jerked open the desk drawer.

At last! I thought.

But instead of what I expected, there were only fingernail clippings, a battery, paper clips, a cigar, and a matchbook from the Figure of Speech Academy of Modeling and Broadcasting in Memphis.

"Dang!" I exclaimed out loud, arousing a sleeping ferret.

"Grrr," it said, baring its pointy teeth.

From outside came the sound of whistling. Mr. Potts was coming home. Closing its deadly mouth, the ferret bounded out to greet him.

"Ah, Finn," Mr. Potts said, dropping his backpack on the table. "Did you sleep well?"

"I guess so," I replied.

Among the items Mr. Potts had brought were milk, coffee, a McDonald's bag, lottery tickets, and a copy of the *Memphis Commercial Appeal*.

How lucky to find such things on the beach, I thought.

"Care for breakfast?" he asked, offering me an Egg McMuffin.

It was still warm.

"Thanks," I said. "But . . ."

With a raised hand, he invalidated my question before I could utter it.

"Eat up," Mr. Potts instructed. "I'm sure you have things to do."

"Well, there is the raft," I answered.

"Ah, the raft," he said, sipping his coffee. "Good luck with that."

The river delivered another sunny day, and soon, with all my chopping, trimming, and lashing, I'd worked up a sweat. Recalling a point where the backwater had formed a lagoon, I decided to cool off with a swim. The tranquil little harbor was clear enough to see catfish browsing its sandy bottom. I stripped to my birthday suit and slipped in.

What a wonderful sensation!

On the bank, ferret heads poked out of burrows. Even though they were as big as adult pigs, I had to laugh. Ferrets of any size can be funny.

One giant would pop up, look around, chitter loudly, then go back down, while another in a hole nearby would appear, like the goofy, hardheaded targets in Whack-a-Mole, next to Skee-Ball my favorite arcade game.

I floated on my back. My, the sun felt good! There's something about drifting between the earth and the sky that puts a person right with the world.

I'm not only free, I thought, *I'm reborn.*

It's a good thing I felt that way, because while I was celebrating life's sweetness, giant ferrets were stealing my clothes.

The Treasure in the Cave

Naked and treading water, I shouted to the thieves on the shore, "Hey, you stinky varmints, stop that!"

Although I'd given it little thought since their shoplifting spree in my willow hut, among the natural traits of these incorrigible polecats is a fondness for petty larceny and pack-ratting. They take people's stuff and stash it in their secret ferret vaults.

In theory, this activity sounds amusing, but when you're scrambling over rocks and running through thorny locust stands as naked as a Kansas jaybird, it's hard to muster up a chuckle.

"Dang you, weasels," I muttered. "Which way did you go?"

I don't how far I traveled, and neither was I certain which way I'd gone, but after more than half an hour of hot pursuit, I had to admit that I was beaten. Blocking the path, a fallen black walnut tree provided a convenient, if somewhat uncomfortable, chair.

Now what do I do? I wondered.

Sometimes I think that fate can read our minds. You know how people like to say that it's always darkest before the dawn, or every time a door shuts, the higher powers get together to pry open a window—that sort of thing?

In my experience, that's often true.

Of course, I prefer the way that Daschell Potts expresses it in *Folderol:* "No matter how many times you try to drown a duckling, it keeps bobbing up again."

Anyway, just when I was feeling defeated, Jim showed up with my shoes.

"Jim!" I cried. "Am I glad to see you!"

"Chi-chi-chi!" Jim responded, laying his treasures on the ground and launching into a back-arching, side-stepping weasel dance.

The laces were totally useless, having been chewed by ferrets into tassels, and the linings were damp, no doubt from feral ferret slobber, but it beat going barefoot, so I slipped the shoes on like moccasins.

"Jim," I asked, "where are my clothes?"

"Chi-chi-chi!" he answered, switching his tail back

and forth like a squirrel in a tree, beckoning for me to follow.

"All right," I told him. "You lead the way."

My faithful ferret friend took me along the river and through the woods and over hill, chip, and dale. Twice we stopped for refreshment—nuts, berries, fresh water from a burbling spring, fat crayfish roasted on an open fire.

I began to imagine myself as one of the first Americans, a native Chickasaw, back before the time of Christopher Columbus, dressed as the Great Spirit had created me, treading gently on the land, communing with the world of animals and plants, taking only what I needed to survive.

Goodness! I was beginning to *think* like Daschell Potts writes.

"*Chi-chi-chi,*" Jim suddenly announced.

To my astonishment, I saw that we were standing at the mouth of a cave. Partially concealed by an outcropping of crumbling limestone and a thick purple patch of vetch, it wasn't a particularly large opening—no bigger than a suburban sewer pipe—but if we ducked down and scrunched our shoulders, it was big enough to admit a teenage boy and his golden retriever–size ferret.

"Way to go, Jim!" I praised, rubbing him behind his rounded, almost nonexistent ears. "You're a good weasel."

Jim rolled onto his back like a well-fed puppy.

The problem with caves is that except for the first fifty feet or so, they're completely dark inside. You need a reliable source of light to explore them. At the time, I didn't even have pants, much less a Coleman lantern or a hefty three-battery steel-encased Maglight, so the best I could do was poke around the foyer.

It was obvious that someone else had been here, however. Dozens of giant ferret tracks, a fresh cigar butt, still smoldering, countless McDonald's wrappers, and an empty bottle of California red wine all suggested that this cave was no secret.

Then I spotted what I thought was a scrap of paper on the floor—a message, perhaps? But when I picked it up, it turned out to be a partially used book of matches from the Figure of Speech Academy of Modeling and Broadcasting in Memphis, Tennessee, just like the one I'd seen in Daschell Potts's desk.

Aha! I concluded. *He's been here!*

Striking one of the matches, I could see that the cave went on for a considerable distance, as did the tracks.

Continuing to strike matches, I followed them until, on my last match, a glint in the pathway caught my eye.

It was a coin!

And not just any coin, mind you. Roughly the size of an old-fashioned silver dollar, it bore the face of a strange-looking man on one side and the raised letter W on the other.

A gold piece! I immediately concluded, my heart pounding with excitement. *Buried treasure!*

Suddenly, to my horror, the last match fizzled out and my whole world plunged into darkness.

Stranger in a Strange Hut

You don't know darkness until you've experienced it inside a cave. The darkness of a cave is complete. Not a ray, not a speck, not a tiny, quark-size particle of illumination from the outside world gets through. Compared to the darkness of a cave, ordinary, run-of-the-mill nighttime is a festival of lights.

Panicked, I dropped the gold coin and groped for the rocks.

Take it easy, Will, I told myself. *Try to look on the bright side.*

At least I could still make myself laugh.

It was also fortunate that I hadn't traveled very far, and luckier still that I remembered which way I'd come. But as I painstakingly inched up the corridor, one chilling thought kept crossing my mind:

What if I get turned around?

It wasn't as if I could just go to bed and wait for the sunrise. If I were truly lost in the belly of the earth, I'd be a goner.

Time, too, gets lost in the darkness. Without the clues provided by ever-changing natural light, in the interior of a cave, our disorientation extends to how long we've been there.

Eventually, after many fearful minutes—or was it hours, who can say?— I found my way outside.

Whew! I thought, collapsing on the ground. *Never again!*

The search for the ferret stash and my clothes would have to wait for another day, and, quite possibly, another searcher.

Rejoining my sidekick, Jim, I hiked to the willow hut, where I planned to pick up clothing and supplies.

Moses had returned, I was happy to see, perched on a branch and looking none too good for his absence. The great blue heron sounded a low, guttural crow-like call of recognition.

"Shhh!" I whispered, returning the greeting with a wave of my hand. "Keep it down. We'll talk later."

In my wardrobe-compromised condition—bare as a newborn babe—I certainly didn't want to call attention to myself. Carefully, I tiptoed to the doorway and listened. It was as silent as a schoolroom on a Saturday afternoon.

I peeked inside.

Nothing.

Slipping furtively inside my own house, I let my eyes adjust to the dimness, a process that worked quickly, thanks to my conditioning in the cave. When the picture snapped into view, I hardly recognized the place. Julia had redecorated my hand-made island habitat from top to bottom.

On the floor was a braided rug. The walls displayed Hello Kitty posters. Cut flowers sprang from tall pink plastic vases.

The look of the bedroom was even more alarming. Julia had fashioned a canopy and draped it with gauze. Where once I'd kept a collection of books that

I'd scavenged there was a display of figurines—uni-corns, butterflies, cherubs, and big-eyed, flop-eared bunnies. Framed photos of recording artists and movie stars stared at me from the chest of drawers.

Good heavens! I thought.

All my clothes were gone. In their place were shorts and tops, cotton dresses, jumpers, plaid skirts, and alien-looking undergarments.

Helping myself to a chocolate candy (orange cream, I discovered happily) from a box by the bed, I searched the rest of the house, finding no sign at all of the previous owner—me.

I'd been gone for only a day, but it was as if I had never lived there at all.

"Isn't this a fine how-do-you-do?" I said to Jim.

Curious, the big ferret poked his nose into a drawer stuffed with knee socks.

From outside came a sharp, insistent squawk.

Was Moses's cranky mate after him again? Or was the wise old water bird warning me of the approach of Julia?

Quickly, I looked for something to put on. Even in such a compelling emergency as this, I had no inten-tion of wearing girls' clothes.

It's ironic, but "thinking fast" doesn't involve

thinking at all. Actually, it's just the opposite. When the heat is on, stopping to weigh your alternatives is the sort of thing that can get you killed. The animal kingdom's top survivors depend on instinct. When danger threatens, they don't think—they react.

Perhaps this explains why, when Julia walked into the bedroom, she found me dressed in floppy tennis shoes and a weasel. The long, furry Jim was draped around my neck like a feather boa, his tail clasped securely between his teeth.

"Good grief, Will!" Julia exclaimed, when the look of horror finally faded from her face. "For a minute there, I thought you were Bigfoot!"

"Julia," I replied, careful to keep Jim from sliding off my shoulders. "Sit down. We have to talk."

A Hardy Boy and Nancy Drew

Sometimes, no matter how foolishly you're dressed, it's best to say what's on your mind.

While not mentioning Mr. Potts, I informed Julia that her self-centered antics had seriously jeopardized my plan to save a priceless manuscript.

I added what a hardship it had been to be forced to

live out-of-doors with insects, snakes, earthworms, and weasels, and how particularly upset I'd been to find that my house had been subjected to Extreme Makeover, Julia Edition.

Throughout this calm but heartfelt complaint, Julia sat silent, examining alternately the curved willow ceiling and her neatly folded hands, but when I got to the part about the discovery of the gold coin in the cave, suddenly she came to life.

"What incredible luck, Will!" Julia exclaimed. "A gold coin? A weird face? The letter *W*? I don't how you did it, but it sounds to me like you've blundered across the buried treasure of Whitebeard!"

"Who?" I asked.

"Whitebeard," she repeated. "The pirate. The infamous Curse of the Caribbean."

"I thought his name was Blackbeard," I said.

"That's a different guy," Julia insisted. "This one had a big bushy beard as white as Santa Claus's."

"Hmmm," I said, not fully convinced. "Why would a Caribbean pirate hide his treasure halfway up the Mississippi River? It seems like a long way to go."

"That's the whole point," Julia said, rolling her eyes at my apparent ignorance. "He didn't want anybody to find it."

"Hmmm," I repeated. "I guess he didn't figure on the ingenuity of a race of giant ferrets."

"Who does?" Julia responded.

At this remark, the previously agreeable Jim glared at Julia and bared his teeth, which had the unfortunate effect of releasing his tail, which in turn rearranged my makeshift costume in such a way as to require an immediate remedy.

In a flash, so to speak, I turned around, hoping to save myself further embarrassment. This maneuver, however, proved to be disastrous, for when Julia got a glimpse of my fully revealed backside, she screamed.

"My stars, Will, show some shame!" she shouted. "I'm not your nurse, for criminy's sake!"

Crawling under the bed, which, incidentally, turned out to be where Julia had shoved my clothes, I reflected on a lifetime of humiliation.

Dear God, I prayed to whatever all-powerful force might be listening, *why can't I just be normal?*

It was a long-felt heartfelt sentiment. But what, honestly, was I asking for? When you take the time to dig deeply enough, you discover that nobody is normal.

Perhaps no one has illustrated this fact so convincingly as Daschell Potts. In *Folderol,* the protagonist, initially a cute, fluffy duckling such as you'd find some Sunday morning in your Easter basket, reaches maturity during his meandering circuit of the pond. When the day arrives that he's a fully grown drake— of a species known as a Gadwall—we learn that not only is he skinny, awkward, and colorless, but he is also incapable of saying "quack," making a loud, disturbing *kack-kack* sound instead, punctuated with an occasional shrill, very unducklike whistle.

Alas, sooner or later, we all exhibit a quirky side.

"Will," the teenage beauty and nemesis addressed me sweetly, "once you're presentable, do you suppose you could show me where that cave is? I'd like to get my hands on the treasure before Duane gets here."

"Who's Duane?" I asked, directing my question to the underside of the mattress where a faded DO NOT REMOVE UNDER PENALTY OF LAW tag was tickling my nose.

"I already told you," Julia said. "He's my boyfriend. He's coming to get me."

"Oh, right," I replied, sneezing. "I forgot."

It was late afternoon when Jim, Julia, and I set out

for the other side of the island. It took a while to round up candles, rope, trail mix, energy bars, bottled water, and a canvas tote bag with leather handles to hold all the loot that Julia expected to find, and then, just as we were about to leave, she decided to change into what she called her spelunker clothes, a purple leotard that made her look like a sack of grapes.

I was wearing a white T-shirt and jeans—a welcome change from ferrets.

"This is so cool," Julia gushed, when at last we were under way. "It's like you're one of the Hardy Boys and I'm Nancy Drew."

"If you say so," I replied.

I hadn't expected the cave to be guarded, but after all I'd already been through, I should have realized that what we don't expect is generally the very thing that's waiting for us. In this case, it was the enormous white ferret, that spooky, red-eyed, chalk-colored behemoth that I'd first observed eating packaged burgers from a one-eared man's outstretched hand.

"Keep your distance," I warned Julia. "I don't like the looks of this guy."

"Finally," my companion replied. "Something we can agree on."

"You go first, I instructed. "I'll cover your flank.""

"You so much as *touch* my flank, William however-many-middle-names-you-have Finn, and you'll wind up being ferret fodder," she threatened. "I'm calling the shots from here on."

"Yes, ma'am," I agreed meekly. "Whatever you say."

The Accidental Spelunker

The sun was going down, but I figured that once you're inside a cave, it makes no difference whether it's night or day. The only thing that matters is who's—or what's—inside there with you.

"Why don't you distract him while I sneak inside," I suggested.

"Me?" Julia answered. "Why don't you? You're the one who's got a way with weasels."

"Yes, but I'm the one who knows where the coin is," I argued. "I can be in and out of there in a jiffy."

"Oh, no," Julia insisted. "We're not going to split up the team. You and I are in this deal together, mister."

The setting sun formed a halo around Julia's hair.

Her eyes appeared to dance in merriment.

What a pretty girl, I thought, and not for the first time.

"All right," I agreed. "Maybe Jim can help."

But when I looked around, I found my faithful ferret pal cowering in the bushes, his head tucked underneath his stomach, like a bird protecting itself in a storm.

"Fat chance," Julia muttered.

"Okay, here's another idea," I announced. "We circle around behind the white ferret, scream into his ears, throw our food into his mouth, then run real fast into the cave."

Julia gave me a look that could have melted steel.

"I hope you're not counting on a career in management," she said.

"What?" I replied.

Several yards away, the big albino beast yawned, revealing a set of teeth like saw blades. He sniffed the air, tilted his head, and cocked in ears in our direction.

"Something's not right about that guy," Julia observed.

"That's for sure," I agreed. "He's as big as a saber-toothed tiger and twice as dangerous."

"No, that's not it," Julia corrected me. "It's something else."

Without warning, Julia leapt from our hiding place and threw her arms above her head, like a referee signaling a touchdown. The red-eyed weasel's expression never changed.

"He's blind!" I whispered.

"Bingo!" Julia replied. "Now, here's my plan: We circle around behind him and slip into the cave one at a time. You go first. Understand?"

"Of course I understand," I told her. "It's a simple variation on *my* plan."

Julia grimaced. "It's nothing like your plan," she insisted. "Your plan was risky, complicated, and fatally flawed."

"It might have worked," I mumbled.

I wouldn't have thought it possible, but the white ferret was even bigger up close. Because he'd placed himself in front of the cave, Julia and I were within an arm's length of the brute. The stink that wafted from his body was stronger than week-old highway skunk.

"Pee-yew!" Julia whispered. "I don't see how you stand it."

"Shhh!" I warned her. "Quiet. He may not be able to see, but there's nothing wrong with his hearing."

As if to illustrate my point, the white ferret stood up, arched his back, and switched his tail like a bull-whip.

Julia and I froze in our tracks.

A tense moment passed, but then the great white weasel's restlessness subsided and his breathing suggested he was sleeping.

"Let's go," I mouthed to Julia, motioning for her to follow. "There's no time to lose."

Once inside, we tied ourselves together with a short length of rope and lit the candles. Shadows leapt along the walls like cockroaches scurrying behind a refrigerator.

"Ugh," Julia said. "This better not take long."

"I dropped it somewhere around here," I explained. "As shiny as gold is, it shouldn't be too hard to find."

Using wax drippings, I stuck my candle to an outcropping and dropped to all fours to sift through the soil. A few feet away, Julia did the same. Outside, the sun had set, the watchdog weasel was sleeping, and the wind was picking up. Occasionally, despite our being far from the breezy entrance, the candles flickered ominously on the wall.

"Find anything?" I asked.

"Yeah, sure," Julia snapped. "A king's ransom. I'm

just crawling around now for the exercise."

We continued our search, with Julia taking one side of the cave while I examined the other. Occasionally, I'd look in her direction.

In the weak candlelight, Julia seemed more beautiful than ever, her head close to the ground, her rear end tilted up like a newly fluffed pillow. However, it's a well-known fact that in near darkness, even without a jukebox playing in the background, men's perception of women frequently slips into an altered state.

Sigh, I sort of breathed, sort of thought, sort of said out loud.

It wasn't only Julia's appearance that held my attention. It was her imperfections, as well. I could tell that she worked to keep her weight down, and that she colored her hair. Sometimes when she spoke, she substituted the words "hopefully," "actually," and "you know," for punctuation. These weren't character flaws, in my opinion. They were beauty marks.

Good heavens, I thought. *It's true what they say about proximity. I'm falling in love with Julia.*

Suddenly, my fingers came into contact with something small, circular, and metallic.

"I've got it!" I cried.

"Let me see," Julia ordered. "Hand it over."

Obediently, I placed the coin in her hand as the wind outside howled like a wild coyote, the white ferret awoke, and the candles suddenly went out.

"Uh-oh," I said.

"What do you mean, 'Uh-oh'?" Julia demanded.

"*Chi-chi-chi!*" the white ferret shrieked, seemingly right behind us.

"What I mean," I shouted in reply, "is run for it!"

The Inner Sanctum

"Run?" she cried, with the giant white ferret closing in on us. "Which way?"

"To the back of the cave!" I hollered, tugging the tethered Julia like a puppy on a leash.

Without being able to see what lies ahead, running in total darkness is nearly impossible. You smash into things: an outcropping, a stalactite, a rock wall. In a cave, the best you can do is an arm-swinging walk.

We didn't slow down for a quarter of an hour, so we must have traveled at least a mile. Fortunately, it was all downhill.

In the pitch black surroundings, the only sound we

heard was the desperate panting of our own breathing.

"I think we lost him," I said.

"Possibly," Julia replied.

"Well, anyway," I pointed out, "he'll never find us now. This place is darker than a black hole in space."

I couldn't tell if the sudden sound of exasperation in my ear was Julia continuing to recover from our marathon or an involuntary expression of her annoyance.

"Wise up, Will Finn!" she snapped. "That weasel-shaped Komodo dragon out there is as blind as a bat. In a world where the light never shines, the blind ferret is king. Got it? Light a freaking candle."

"Okay," I agreed. "Give me one."

"Do what?" Julia asked, ice forming on the edge of her words.

"Give me a candle and I'll light it," I repeated patiently. "I've got a book of matches right here in my pocket."

"But no candles," Julia said.

"No," I confirmed, adopting the careful, measured tone of a kindergarten teacher. "I have the matches. I gave you the candles."

"You gave me a coin," Julia insisted. "You never gave me any candles."

Hmmm, I thought.

"Never mind," I told her. "We'll just find our way out of here using the fire in your eyes."

It was then that my relationship with Julia reached its lowest point. Roped to me as we stood side by side in a damp passageway halfway to the center of the earth, with a foul-smelling, sumo wrestler–size carnivore sniffing at one end and a bottomless pit to the devil's hacienda at the other, the sweaty Julia hauled off and slugged me.

"Ow!" I cried, falling over a rock, an action that pulled the rope taut, jerking my assailant toward me. Like Jack and Jill, we tumbled down an incline, landing in a puddle, Julia's head on my shoulder.

"Why did you do that?" I asked.

Even under such extreme circumstances, I couldn't help but notice Julia's appealing scent, a blend of perfume and perspiration that made me dizzy.

Or had I merely hit my head?

"You are such an idiot," Julia said. "How many matches do you have?"

"I don't know," I answered. "Half a book or so, I guess."

"Light one," she demanded.

Fumbling in my pocket, I retrieved the matchbook from the Figure of Speech Academy of Modeling and Broadcasting in Memphis.

"Gee, I hope they're not wet," I said.

"Grrr," Julia snarled.

One paper match doesn't seem like much, but when your eyes are dilated, it's remarkably effective, if only for a moment. Somehow, Julia and I had stumbled into a subterranean storage vault, a secret cache stacked floor to ceiling with loot. The dimly lit tableau reminded me of the hideout of Ali Baba and the forty thieves.

"Hey!" I exclaimed. "That's my remote control!"

"Those are my barrettes!" Julia chimed in. "And that's my silver mirror, my bath mat, and my slotted spoon!"

So! I thought. *So this is where the ferrets stash their ill-gotten gains!*

"What's that over there?" I asked, pointing to an object by the wall.

"It looks like a pirate's chest," Julia replied, just as the match sputtered out.

Once again sentenced to total darkness, Julia and I reached out to hold hands. Her grip was steady. Her palm was soft. I could feel her pulse running through it.

Or was it my own?

From somewhere far away, the sound of an angry ferret echoed through the cave.

"Chi-chi-chi-fo-fum," it seemed to be saying.

"You know," I said to Julia, "man has always been at the mercy of predators. Bears, sharks, tigers, alligators, giant squids, anacondas, pterodactyls, wolves— the list goes on and on."

"William Alexander Madison Lee Cooper Finn," Julia spoke with great precision. "Listen carefully to what I'm telling you: Light . . . another . . . match."

Psssst!

The tiny yellow flame sprang to life.

Once again the pirate chest flickered into view, but as I was lifting its lid, Julia was staring into her hand.

"This isn't a gold piece," she declared. "And that's not a *W*. You were holding it upside down. It's a capital *M*—the Golden Arches. And the face on the other side isn't some Spanish king or Italian nobleman, it's that stupid white-faced, big-footed clown from TV, Ronald McDonald!

"Will—you everlasting idiot—this is a Happy Meal prize!"

With that assessment, my companion flung the coin at my head. Miraculously, I caught it.

"Chi-chi-grrr-yeek!" the white ferret screamed from somewhere down the corridor.

Oh, man! I thought.

Clearly, the pressure was mounting. But this time, just before the match snuffed out, I snatched up an armload of papers from the trunk.

At last, I thought. *I have the key to the future: Daschell Potts's secret manuscript!*

Commotion in the Hall

Ferrets once roamed in vast numbers in America, happily feeding off an excess of fat, chattering prairie dogs. But then, at the insistence of ranchers who considered the docile rodents to be "vermin," no better than rats, bedbugs, or horseflies, the federal government got into the act, gassing innocent prairie dogs in their underground homes by the millions. Today, the black-footed ferret teeters on extinction. It is the North American continent's single most endangered mammal.

Little wonder, then, that Mother Nature decided to

fight back, creating a ferret species with individuals up to fifty times the size of the original. That some of them should also be angry is, under the circumstances, entirely understandable.

Unfortunately, at that particular moment, I could think of no way to express my sympathy to the furious predator coming down the hall. Inadvertently, I feared, Julia and I had become a meal additive known as Prairie Dog Helper. Literally and figuratively, our backs were against the wall.

"I don't who I'm more disappointed in," Julia said. "You or Duane."

She was referring to her high school boyfriend, who thus far had failed to materialize.

"Well," I replied, "at least I'm here to get you out of this jam."

"True," Julia agreed, "but then, you're the one who got me into it."

"I remember a short story from English class," I said.

"You're *not* planning to tell it to me *now?*" she asked.

"I'll summarize," I said.

"*Chi-chi-chi!*" came the hungry-sounding echo from far down the corridor.

"A man was in a jungle about to be eaten by a tiger," I recounted. "He looked up and saw a piece of low-hanging fruit. Just before the tiger leapt on him, the man plucked the fruit and bit into it. His last thought—and the last line in the story—was 'How good it tasted.'"

"'How good it tasted'!" Julia repeated. "That's it? The guy is about to buy the farm and that's the only thing he can think of to do? Where did you go to school, Will? The moon? And what kind of lame-brained story is *that?*"

"It's a famous story," I explained. "I wish I could remember who wrote it. I know it wasn't Daschell Potts. He uses bigger words."

"It's a stupid story," Julia muttered.

"Come here, Julia," I insisted, mustering up all the courage in my being to reach out and pull her toward me.

Fumbling in the darkness, I planted a kiss on my invisible companion, initially missing her mouth and making contact with her salty, high-boned cheek, then sliding over to her painted lips, where, to my astonishment and delight, she not only accepted the slight, sudden pressure but returned it in kind.

If there'd been any light at all, it would have

revealed an image like a close-up in a movie, where two impassioned lovers, separated by a world at war, are at last reunited.

This was no mere peck. It was a long, lingering mouthful of the real thing.

How good it tasted!

In a flash, the blind ferret was on my back, his thirty-four sharp teeth clamped onto my arm. Clearly my brain was in good working order: The pain was instantaneous.

"Take this," I gasped, giving Julia the priceless Potts manuscript. "Now get out of here. I'll hold him off as long as I can."

"Are you sure?" she whimpered. "What if . . ."

"Go!" I interrupted, pressing the book of matches into her hand. "And use these to find your way."

By now the white ferret had me pinned to the cave floor, a bearlike, claw-bearing paw on each of my shoulders, his small but lethal mouth mere inches from my neck.

Boy, does this guy's breath stink! I thought.

"Listen," I whispered to the ferret, trying not to show my desperation. "I'm sorry for your disability— I really am—but that's no excuse for turning me into some kind of Big Mac with Cheese."

People who keep them as pets report that ferrets are unusually smart. Ferrets quickly learn their names. They're readily housebroken. They can be taught to do any number of complex tricks. Ferrets are said to be more loyal than cats and cleverer than dogs. The great divide between humans and animals is speech, but given the chance, ferrets, I'm told, like dogs, dolphins, chimpanzees, elephants, pot-bellied pigs, and parrots, can recognize dozens—and possibly hundreds—of words.

Apparently, to the white ferret, I'd accidentally spoken two of these.

When I uttered the magic words "Big Mac," the white ferret became as gentle as a kitten, nuzzling my cheek, licking my hand, even purring—after a fashion.

So that's it, I thought. *Whatever Daschell Potts's secret plan is, it has something to do with McDonald's!*

Lady Wildfire

The thing about animals in the wild is that they don't have anybody they can trust. There's always someone

89

after their habitat, their food supply, their pelts, their horns, their hooves, their claws, their teeth, their ears, their glands, their testicles, their babies, their poor, sad, emaciated carcasses.

Deep inside the cave, I tentatively reached out in the darkness and scratched the sightless giant ferret behind his saucer-shaped ears. His fur was incredibly soft—deep, rabbitlike, downy, and comforting, like a favorite blanket from years gone by.

"It's okay," I told him. "If you're not mad at me, I'm not mad at you."

"*Chi-chi-chi,*" he said.

From an animal's point of view, most people are no damn good. Not only do I understand this way of thinking, but I agree with it. In just about any human/critter matchup you'd care to name, I'd most likely side with the animal.

Even though the ferret beside me was as big as a bighorn sheep, in the great scheme of the modern, man-made world, he was the odd man out, a perpetual underdog, a full-time fugitive.

I sat with him in the darkness for a long time, scratching his stomach until my arm got tired. When I was pretty sure that he wasn't going to devour me, I carefully climbed onto his long, limber back, clutched his fur with both hands, and spoke softly into his ear.

"Home," I instructed. "Let's go home."

The blind ferret stood up and began to walk toward the cave entrance at a steady, deliberate pace, his back rising and falling, causing me to lurch left and right, left and right, left and right, until, within a very few minutes, I was seasick.

This must be what's it's like to ride a camel, I thought.

Adding to my discomfort was the aroma inside the cave. I could see nothing, of course, but the more progress that the blind ferret and I made, the stronger was the overpowering scent of smoke, as if a troop of suburban Boy Scouts had recently built a campfire without a chimney.

Daschell Potts? I wondered. *Is he around here somewhere? He's crazy enough to do this.*

Soon the smoldering in the corridor was making me cough. It didn't smell like the discharge from Mr. Potts's cigars, that stinky-sweet smell reminiscent of dirty socks, wild honey, English Leather cologne, and burning leaves. It was more like an office wastebasket that had caught on fire, or possibly an abandoned squirrel nest stuck in a seldom-used fireplace, or maybe even a poorly executed controlled combustion experiment in a seventh grade science lab, like the time Coach Worgul nearly set the school on fire with his portable hibachi and we all got to go home early.

What a great day that was! I remembered.

Whatever its source, the smoke was thick, cloying, and overbearing, and it didn't begin to dissipate until the white ferret, shaking his head and sneezing, reached the faint light at the end of the tunnel.

"Good boy," I said, coughing hard and blinking the acrid, airborne particles from my teary eyes. "You've saved us."

Dismounting, I gave the white ferret a nuzzle and a pat as Jim bounded up to demand his share of the same.

It was nighttime and cloudless. The stars seemed extraordinarily bright. A sliver of a moon grinned like Lewis Carroll's now-you-see-me, now-you-don't Cheshire cat. From the shadows, the minxlike, Spandex-clad Julia sidled up and greeted me with a hug.

"Oh, Will," she gushed. "I was so worried about you."

Her hair smelled of shampoo and smoke. On her cheek, just below her ear, I felt a soft, fine layer of duckling down.

"We'd better get out of here," I whispered urgently. "Where's the manuscript?"

"Are you serious?" Julia responded, stepping back to eye me with a quizzical look. "I used it, just like you told me to."

"What do you mean, you used it?" I asked.

"To find my way out of the cave, Will," she replied. "What do think I mean?"

"What?" I cried. "You burned the manuscript? No! Tell me it isn't so!"

"Not all at once," Julia replied. "Just a few pages at a time, and only until I was safely outside. Oh, Will! How clever of you to think of it. I could see quite clearly."

"Aaargh!" I hollered, throwing myself at her feet and pounding my fists on the ground.

"Oh, for Pete's sake, Will, pull yourself together!" Julia admonished. "From the way you're behaving, you'd think I'd just incinerated the treasure."

A Nefarious Plan

Six pages of Mr. Potts's manuscript had been spared from Julia's foolish torchlight.

Six measly pages.

Six typewritten, double-spaced, eight-and-a-half-by-eleven-inch pages. A single postage stamp's sampling of all the years of Mr. Potts's brilliant ruminations, half a dozen flimsy paper fragments from a priceless collection of never-to-be-equaled human achievement.

This was a situation that exceeded catastrophe. This was a literary wrong so great that my mind could not fathom it.

"Julia," I said, with a heavy heart, and a long, sad sigh. "You're pretty. But you're not *that* pretty."

"I don't see what the big deal is," she replied. "You can't miss what you never had."

You couldn't be more wrong, I thought.

In Mr. Potts's only published masterpiece, *Folderol,* the duckling's journey around the pond is a metaphorical quest for what's lacking in his life, and nothing is going to stop him until he finds it.

Missing what we've never had is the main reason to go on living.

I had come so close.

I'd held Mr. Potts's manuscript in my very own hands. Now all that was left was half a chapter and a trail of death gray ashes.

Although it was still too dark to read, a faint glow just below the horizon suggested that sunrise wasn't far away.

"Why don't you head back home," I suggested to Julia. "Maybe I'll catch up with you later."

"Take your time," Julia replied, yawning. "I'm going to bed."

If you've ever watched a photograph being developed in a darkroom, then you know what it was like to be staring at Mr. Potts's few pages while the sun rounded the edge of the earth. Gradually, like a chemical reaction, the words came into view, words I'd seen before, but whose meaning escaped me until now. Seeing them in this context, I felt myself chilled to the bone.

"We attack at dawn," it began.

> Deploying our trained team of giant killer ferrets, packed into a yellow school bus, we will attack the McDonald's in Clarksdale, then move north, refining our methods in Lula, Tunica, Lake Cormorant, and Glover, before we unleash maximum force on the newly renovated McDonald's in midtown

Memphis. We are heartened by the fact that we have the advantage of both size and surprise.

Holy smokes! I thought.

The remainder of the pages detailed team member assignments, with ferrets identified by name, most bearing innocent-sounding monikers such as Toby, Bogey, Baxter, Ben, Harley, Big Tucker, Little Tucker, Cleo, Chloe, Winky, Maggie, Woody, Lola, Sassy, Larry, Milton, Tommy, Eddie, and Muffin. But even though it read like the graduation roster from the puppy training class at PetSmart, it was in fact an itemization of an army of very large, ruthless killers.

This was no novel Daschell Potts had been working on. This was an evildoer's manifesto—a twisted plan for pop-cultural terrorism concocted by a madman!

McDonald's?

With giant ferrets?

Why, it was even worse than if he'd planned to kidnap Britney Spears and force her to dress up in Amish clothes!

But why? I wondered.

What had happened to the great Daschell Potts, famous author and role model for millions, to turn him from the world's most admired literary genius into a demented fast food activist, a deranged and dangerous eco-terrorist?

The answer, no doubt, had been incinerated by the impulsive hand of my new best friend, Julia.

Dang, girl! I thought. *And just when we were start-ing to get along!*

By now, the sky was a series of alternating crimson, turquoise, and magenta stripes, like a Navajo blanket, handwoven from dust, light, and water vapor. The sight held me spellbound. No matter how many times I see the sunrise, I always pause to receive the eternal promise of dawn.

Dawn? I repeated in my mind.

"We attack at dawn," Mr. Potts had declared.

Good heavens! I thought. *What if today's the day?*

There was one way to find out: Look for ferrets. If the gargantuan carnivores were still on the island, then perhaps I had time to act. If they were gone, then the river towns of the north Mississippi and the unsuspecting sleepy backwater city of Memphis, just across the border in the state of Tennessee, were in for the second biggest surprise of their placid southern lives (the first having occurred between the years of 1861 and 1865, in case you were wondering).

"Jim!" I shouted. "Where are you?"

Immediately, a responsive crash echoed through the woods and the big sable ferret came hopping through the underbrush like a hound dog summoned to breakfast.

"Attaboy, Jim," I said, scratching his head. "At least Mr. Potts hasn't succeeded in recruiting *you*."

Figuring it was the first place I'd better check, I set off for Mr. Potts's bottle house. It was a cool, crisp morning, with sumac and Virginia creeper already turning red. Soon, I realized, the cottonwoods would yellow and curl, then the elms and the oaks.

How did I know this?

Frankly, I surprised myself at how completely I'd taken to outdoor life. For as long as I could remember, I'd been hostage to electronic entertainment, dependent on flickering screens to feed my thoughts. Now I reached into the branches of a pawpaw tree and plucked out my breakfast.

Ah, freedom! I thought.

As with the sunrise, there's just no getting over it.

It's not that my previous life was bad, or that what I was doing now was good. In fact, these distinctions didn't apply to my present circumstances. I was just following the path that was unfolding before me.

Unlike some people I could name.

Unlike Mr. Potts.

Where did he go wrong? I wondered.

Here he had this perfectly wonderful island all to himself, and now he winds up as crazy as a loon.

How did Daschell Potts become the Lord of the Ferrets?

The Ferrets Are Coming! The Ferrets Are Coming!

I could not shake off the question. What had happened to Daschell Potts?

How had this once great man fallen into such a sorry state of mind?

Why had he chosen to exchange the adoring company of the world's nobility for the foul and fickle companionship of very fat ferrets?

Had Daschell Potts suffered a blow to the head?

Had his early, unexpected fame upset him so much that he sought the company of these monsters simply for protection?

Is there ever a point at which there is a logical explanation for lunacy?

And where was Daschell Potts at this moment?

Hiding in the cave?

Attacking a group of Quarter-Pounder fanciers in the ragged cotton fields and shallow catfish farms of Lula, Mississippi?

One thing seemed certain. Daschell Potts was literally engaged in the act of biting the hand that fed him, leading a bizarre band of giant, carnivorous weasels—as if he were John Singleton Mosby with his feared guerrilla raiders—The Gray Ghost—in sneak attacks on rural, roadside, and presumably undeserving McDonald's restaurants.

Perhaps when he lost his ear to the ferret bite, some of his brains spilled out as well.

I could think of no other explanation.

Just ahead of me, shining in the morning sun like a great magic crystal, casting multicolored rays in all directions, sat Merlin's own spacecraft in the woods —Daschell Potts's bottle house, built entirely from empty wine, beer, and whiskey bottles.

Had he consumed each individually, one at a time, or acquired a truckload of empties, as you'd order patio stone or garden mulch from Home Depot?

There were no ferrets lounging in the yard—a worrisome sign. Neither did I encounter any inside the house—only a dirt-floored room strewn with discarded hamburger wrappers, as if a whirlwind had touched down on the trash dumpster behind McDonald's.

This wasn't like the tidy Mr. Potts I'd met when I first arrived on Ferret Island. Either he'd been in a big hurry to leave, or, of greater concern, the deranged master plotter wasn't planning to come back at all.

Yikes! I thought. *I have to warn somebody.*

Racing to my willow house as fast as the tangled woods would permit, I called for my former room-mate the moment I reached the clearing.

"Julia!" I screamed. "Hurry. We've got to get out of here!"

But the only reply was the rustling of the cotton-wood leaves.

Julia, too, was missing.

A frantic, heart-racing inspection of my regular island haunts turned up no more ferrets, no more authors, no more castaway girls. Only a colony of interior least terns nesting on the beach near my unfinished raft.

"Excuse me, fellows," I said to the chronically beleaguered water birds, "I hate to disturb you, but you're sitting right where I need to launch."

As an endangered species, the little terns had become accustomed to being shoved aside for mankind's more pressing activities, including, and ironically for this specific group, the clearing of land for the construction of a new McDonald's indoor playground in nearby Shelby, Mississippi.

Dutifully, without changing expression, the fifteen yellow-footed, orange-beaked underdogs trotted to the far end of the beach.

"Thanks," I said.

Although not completed according to its original Potts-provided specifications—the handmade water-craft was maybe six logs shy of a comfortable ride—it seemed to me to be seaworthy enough. If Jim sat at one end and I sat at the other, once we got out into the current we were bound to go ashore somewhere.

Anyway, I told myself, *there comes a time when you have to act.*

How did the duckling put it in *Folderol*?

"The difference between failure and success is a pin-feather's worth of courage," it said.

Knowing nothing about river navigation, I took my Swiss Army knife and cut a pole from a sapling, dragged the raft into the lagoon, and then, pushing, pulling, and coaxing, got the trembling Jim aboard.

To say that he was reluctant to go sailing is putting it mildly. Clearly the big galoot was frightened of the water.

Hmmm, I thought. *Maybe ferrets can't swim.*

Shoving off, the narrow raft tilted under Jim's weight to the point where his tail became submerged, trailing behind us like a fishing line. Jim put his head down on the logs and looked up at me with desperate black eyes.

"Hang in there, pal," I told him. "This is just a temporary inconvenience."

Our progress was slow. The sapling was useful for propelling us only as long as it reached the sandy bottom, a situation that changed twenty feet from shore. Now we found ourselves at the mercy of the breeze and the meandering current. From here on, we could control our direction only with the use of the rudder.

The rudder! I realized. *That's what's missing!*

Why didn't Mr. Potts mention a rudder?

Good grief! I realized. *There's no way to steer!*

Once Again, into the Drink

Events astonish me.

I swear, they have lives of their own.

This did not start out to be the story of a boy and his ferret pal trapped on a jerry-rigged raft in the middle of America's widest, swiftest river with no way to steer, even if he knew how, which, of course, he—that is, I—didn't.

It was supposed to be just a simple, uneventful bus ride to the easygoing southern city of Memphis to visit my stepgrandmother, Nana, until things cooled off back home in Kansas City.

But have you noticed?

One thing always leads to another. And most times, where it leads is not where you thought you were going.

All I can say is, if you're going to try to get by in this world, I hope you like surprises.

One minute Jim and I were basking like summer sunbathers on a floating dock in a pretty country lake. The next minute we were out to sea, so to speak, seized by the powerful and deadly currents of the mighty Mississippi River, its muddy waters sweeping us in ever-widening circles.

"Here we go, Jim!" I cried. "There's no turning back now!"

Jim opened his mouth and let out a bloodcurdling cry.

"Chi-chi-chi!" he screamed.

Holy smokes, I thought. *I had no idea he'd be this scared.*

But it wasn't fear of the swirling whirlpool that set the big ferret's siren off. Something had grabbed his tail.

Thrashing behind us like a Mercury outboard motor, its bony jaws locked on to the tip of my raft-mate's drifting, furry appendage, was what I could have sworn was a shark.

Death white and emaciated, like a living fossil, it was as big as the hapless oversize weasel it had chosen for its prey.

"Great Zeus on Olympus!" I shouted. "It's a pallid sturgeon!"

Like the rare terns we'd inadvertently bothered on the beach, the pallid sturgeon is an endangered species. But unlike those timid little flit-twitterers, this prehistoric fish once ruled its habitat as the undisputed king of the underwater beasts, thriving in the slimy muck of the river bottom to grow as big as a Canadian lumberjack.

The few sturgeons that survive in the Mississippi River today recall the ancient age of dinosaurs, so fearsome and foreign is their appearance—and behavior. And yet, as skeletal-looking as these gaunt, pointy-nosed monsters are, they don't have bones in their bodies. Like their ocean-dwelling cousins the sharks, they're cartilaginous creatures—and certainly every bit as ravenous.

If I hadn't been clinging to a raft in the river, I would have shouted, "Run for your life!"

As it happened, I may as well have set off on foot, because once Jim heaved his big body forward to try to get away from his aquatic attacker, the raft began to break apart.

I don't get it, I said to myself, suddenly treading water and grasping for a bobbing log. *I built it exactly as Mr. Potts instructed.*

"Chi-chi-chi!" cried Jim, his legs astride the separating halves of the raft, his captive tail continuing to tow the horrid, hungry sturgeon.

Even above the rush of the river and the creaking, cracking logs I could hear that sturgeon chomping away, smacking his nasty sturgeon lips as he did so.

Poor Jim! I thought. *He's probably feeling a lot like Captain Hook with the crocodile.*

No, that's not right, I realized.

It's the one-eared Mr. Potts who's the crazy Captain Hook of this unfolding story. Because unless I'd overlooked something, the great author Daschell Potts had deliberately sabotaged me and doomed my ferret friend to a gruesome death!

Of course, what I had overlooked was the fundamental nature of the reclusive genius himself. Anybody who would turn loose a bunch of giant, man-eating ferrets on a swell place like McDonald's has some serious character flaws.

It was at that precise moment that I learned one of life's most important lessons: Just because someone is famous for writing a great book does not necessarily mean that he is a nice person.

"Glug, glug!" gurgled Jim, slipping from the raft and sinking like a mossy stone.

Dang! I thought. *This was a mistake. Can anything save us now?*

Friends in Need

As I felt myself slipping underwater for the third time, my life did not flash before me.

You can forget about that old sailor's tale. Or perhaps I'm not old enough to have accumulated sufficient experience to make for a meaningful life flash.

What did flash before me, however, was the pretty

face of my accidental island colleague, Julia. It's funny how you can live with somebody and still know very little about her.

At a very young age, Julia Tufts was on national TV week after week playing Becky on *Hannigan's Island,* a role that required her to be an accomplished swimmer. When the show finally went kaput, through no fault of her own, I'm sure, she continued to maintain her mastery of the water, twice becoming state champion in Arkansas and captain of her school swim team in Marmaduke.

I would have known this if I'd ever bothered to ask her about herself, but unfortunately I had been too preoccupied with pursuing the latter-day musings of the legendary author and suspected lunatic Daschell Potts.

I've said it before and I'll say it again: Our brains are just too small to know what's really going on.

As it turned out, I was not imagining Julia's face.

She corralled my neck with one muscular arm while she struck out for shore with the other, kicking her feet and moving through the turbulent firmament like a dolphin.

Her arrival in the nick of time may seem an unlikely coincidence, but when you consider how fragile life is, and all the dangers that we face every day, anything that keeps us around for another twenty-four hours is remarkably fortuitous. To my way of thinking, every day is a series of coincidences.

Besides, she'd been watching from the riverbank.

"So," she gasped, paddling me to safety, "you were planning to leave without me."

"Not at all," I insisted, spitting out half a gallon of oily river water. "I looked for you, but you were gone."

"You are such a lying weasel," Julia charged. "You're worse than Duane."

Weasel? I thought.

Jim!

"Wait!" I sputtered. "We can't leave Jim to drown."

"I'm sorry, Will," Julia answered, continuing her steady stroke, "but I've got my hands full at the moment."

The reason clichés show up in daily discourse so frequently is because, time and time again, they prove themselves to be true. Consider the expression "I get by with a little help from my friends." Whereas family is a lasting bond of a particular sort, it's friendship that's the rescuing force in our lives.

In Jim's case, this popular platitude was proved by the arrival of Moses.

They don't call them great blue herons for nothing. These are very big birds, with a wingspan of five or six feet, stalky legs with clawlike toes, and a long, sharp serrated beak that resembles a medieval sword.

There's another amazing fact of animal morphology that I should mention: Ferrets' whiskers, which extend from both sides of their ratty snouts, grow to lengths that exceed that of their heads, which are already longer than a full-grown dachshund's. Black, coarse, and unusually strong, these wiry feelers resemble high-test fishing line. Indeed, if I'd thought about it at the time, I would have lashed the logs together with knotted weasel whiskers rather than the rotted cotton twine that so quickly failed.

Moses dispatched the astonished pallid sturgeon with a single surgical peck to the head, grasped Jim's whiskers with his prehensile toes, and, flapping his enormous wings with all the strength the brave bird's five-pound body could muster, pulled the waterlogged ferret bouncing and skimming across the water like a thrill-seeking tourist clinging to a parasail.

Soggy and exhausted, yet overjoyed, the four of us were reunited on the beach, where, once again, the beleaguered terns determined it best to skitter off to a new location.

Julia extended her arms, possibly to give me a hug, but, stupidly, I shook her hand instead.

"Thanks," I told her. "I owe you one."

"That you do, buster," Julia replied.

Satisfied that the situation was under control, Moses raised his wings like an angel, flapped once, ascended, and soared away over the treetops, his majestic silhouette haloed with magic autumn light.

What a great bird, I thought.

That was when I caught a glimpse of an old man's face peering out from the bushes.

It had to be Daschell Potts!

"Quick, Julia!" I whispered. "After him!"

"Quick, yourself," Julia replied. "I'm beat. In case you didn't notice, I just swam the channel for both of us."

"But it's Mr. Potts!" I explained. "He'll get away."

"And?" Julia answered. "You're suggesting that's a bad thing?"

"Wait here," I instructed.

Every stage in life has its advantages. Babies get coddled. Toddlers get toys. Preschoolers can watch TV all day. Third-graders are excused from housework. Fifth-graders have birthdays that can go on for a week. And by the time you're old enough to attend junior high, you're physically fitter than the adults in charge of your life.

Despite nearly drowning in the Mississippi River, I could still run faster than any old man.

I took off after him.

"Mark my words, Will," Julia called after me. "You'll be sorry if you don't stop now."

The Strange Visitor

Within two minutes, I'd tackled the guy who'd been spying on us, and, to my profound astonishment, discovered that he wasn't Mr. Potts.

"Ooof!" the man said when he fell to the ground. "Ow! You hurt me!"

"Sorry," I said. "But who the heck are you and why were you spying on me?" I demanded, brushing dirt from my elbows.

"Narf," the old man replied.

"Don't bark at me, mister!" I demanded. "Tell me who you are and what you're up to or I'll sic my ferret on you!"

Unfortunately, this was obviously an empty threat. The poor worn-out, waterlogged Jim lay on the riverbank like a wet beach towel with half his furry ferret tail gone, an appetizer for a hungry prehistoric sturgeon.

With great dignity, the old man stood erect and combed his gray hair back with his fingertips.

"I, sir," my captive replied imperially, "am the Honorable Pierre 'Hercules' Narf, the twice-elected representative to the Congress of the United States of America for the fine citizens of the fourth district— Crawdad Parish—of the sovereign state of Louisiana."

"Your Excellency," I responded, bowing as people in the movies do when they find themselves in the presence of royalty, noting as I did so that much like Daschell Potts the gentleman smelled strongly of alcoholic beverages. "A thousand pardons."

"One is sufficient," he muttered.

"Did you fall off the excursion boat from Memphis?" I asked. "I did and so did that girl down there. It seems to be a fairly common problem. Since you're a legislator, maybe you could get a law passed that will put a stop to such accidents."

"Listen, kid," Congressman Narf replied, "I don't

have time for chitchat. I'm on the trail of a missing person, a mean-spirited one-eared man who calls himself Potts. Hangs out with a bunch of hungry overgrown muskrats."

Hmmm, I wondered. *Should I tell him?*

"Who's your friend, Will?" Julia asked, appearing at my elbow and wringing river water from her hair.

"This is Congressman Narf," I told her. "He's looking for Mr. Potts—I mean, some unknown person."

"Aha!" the Congressman exclaimed. "So you've seen him!"

"Are you talking about Will's pal the one-eared weasel shepherd?" Julia asked disingenuously. "Sure, he was here. But that was ages ago. I think he said he had business in Tuscaloosa, Alabama."

"Tuscaloosa!" Narf replied. "So that's where he's taken his little road show."

Road show? I thought. *That's a clever way to put it!*

Without saying thanks or goodbye, the congressman departed the way he'd come.

"Why'd you tell him that?" I said, confronting Julia. "He might have been able to get us off the island."

"I didn't like his looks," Julia explained.

"But he works for the United States government," I said.

"Yeah?" Julia answered. "So do the people in charge of this stupid river, not to mention hurricane preparation. A lot of good those doofuses have done us."

I've said it before and I'll probably say it again. It's too bad our brains are not larger. If they were, perhaps we could remember more things.

For example, if I'd been provided with the cranial storage capacity, I would have recalled that the same issue of *Parade* magazine that erroneously reported that Daschell Potts was a casualty at the hands of Canadian fossil poachers in western Kansas, and that former child star Julia Tufts was captain of her swim team in Marmaduke, Arkansas, had also carried the news that the *former* Louisiana congressman Pierre "Hercules" Narf was serving a prison term in Forrest City, Arkansas.

Alas, we are doomed to be merely human, a thought that somehow brings me back to Julia. Despite her being dripping wet, disrespectful, and fundamentally dishonest, I couldn't get over how attractive she was.

"Listen, Julia," I said, recklessly taking her into my confidence. "Mr. Potts is on a mission to destroy the world—or a small portion of it, anyway. I don't know why, and I don't know exactly how, but I do know this: We've got to stop him before it's too late."

"Sounds okay to me," Julia replied. "I'm getting tired of waiting around for Duane to show up."

Tactfully downplaying the burned-up manuscript issue, I told her what I'd figured out so far.

"Why, your guy's a class-A nutcase," Julia concluded. "A real fit-me-for-a-straitjacket wacko. But then, you knew that, right?"

"Well," I admitted, "I did suspect that being a literary genius, Mr. Potts was probably what you might call quirky."

"Well, there you go, then," Julia said knowingly.

"But how did he get off the island?" I asked. "There's no boat. I've searched. And even if there were a boat, how could he get all the ferrets on it? As big as they are, and as many of them as there are, they couldn't possibly fit on anything smaller than the *Memphis Empress*. And as we've just witnessed, ferrets are terrible swimmers. So what's the explanation? Are they hiding in the cave?"

"It's not a cave," Julia announced.

116

The Ferrorist Underground

On Ferret Island, many were the nights that I had trouble sleeping. Tossing and turning, I never could get comfortable. Was it worries? Mosquitoes? The itchy and scratchy mattress of twigs and leaves? A stomachache brought on by unripe berries?

It took me a while to figure it out.

Our brains, it seems, pay attention to many more things than we do. The conscious mind is but a part-time, underachieving, lazy goof-off, an excuse-making wannabe pitted against the submerged body part that does the real heavy lifting: the subconscious.

Among other things, something was amiss with my hearing, or, more precisely, there was something that I could no longer hear.

The quiet was overwhelming.

At first I thought the white sounds of the rippling river were suppressing the noises of the night, but eventually, with a series of insistent nudges from my subconscious, I realized that what was missing was much more significant than the occasional birdcall, catfight, car crash, or thoughtless neighbor's backyard party.

It was trains.

In the Midwest, where I come from, whether you live in a city, or a town, or out in the country, you're never more than a few miles from a two-hundred-car freight train rumbling down the track, a diesel-powered, cast-iron clattering behemoth hauling rusty containers tagged with spray-painted foreign symbols and jammed to the brim with toys and big-screen TVs and poly-bagged cypress mulch, moving lickety-split from hither to yon, all across the land, all day and all night.

It's the sort of noise that makes newcomers flinch and mongrel dogs bark, but for those of us who've grown up with these low, invisible whistles routinely piercing the gloom, they're a pat on the hand, a kiss on the cheek, a whispered good night, a mother's lullaby.

On the river there are no trains, only barges, and it was the absence of the iron horse's acoustic evidence that was keeping me awake. Even so, for the longest time, my conscious mind was asleep to this now patently obvious fact.

Similarly, inside the cave where I'd discovered the gold coin and the priceless Daschell Potts manuscript, now rendered into a somewhat less valuable trail of ashes by you-know-who, my conscious mind failed to perceive certain physical facts that to my subconscious had been as plain as a ferret's sharp fingernails.

In this case, the role of my subconscious was performed by my hypercritical accidental companion, Julia, the above-mentioned you-know-who.

"It's not a cave," she repeated. "While I was torching those precious pages of yours, I could see that the whole thing looked like it had been hollowed out with toy shovels. It isn't a natural formation, Will. Someone or something dug it."

"You're kidding!" I said.

But even as I attempted this defense, I saw in my mind's eye the thousands upon thousands of identical concave scratches of which she spoke.

"I don't kid, Will Finn—at least, not so you'd notice," she replied. "If you want my guess, I'd say it was the handiwork of ferrets. Anyway, however it got there, it isn't a cave. It's a tunnel. And as any Hardy Boy or Nancy Drew will tell you, unlike caves, which can be blind alleys, tunnels always lead somewhere."

"Under the river," I whispered, amazed.

"And through the woods," Julia added.

"To Nana's house in Memphis," I concluded. "Julia, we have to go back!"

"'Have to'?" Julia quoted me. "That all depends,

don't you think? It's dark in there. Not to mention cold, scary, and unnaturally wet. And I, for one, am out of pages to burn."

I grimaced at this reminder.

"Listen, Julia," I said. "We don't have much time. Mr. Potts has trained those ferrets to kill people. He's taken one of nature's finest species and, by sacrificing his own ear, turned them into a dedicated team of ferrorists—dangerous, bloodthirsty, bandit-faced marauders.

"While you and I are standing here arguing, those brainwashed mustelid monsters of his are munching their way through the unsuspecting customers of McDonald's restaurants from Yazoo City, Mississippi, to Memphis, Tennessee."

"Oh, come on now," Julia interjected. "Why would Mr. Potts want to do that?"

"I'm not sure," I replied. "It may be he's trying to settle some weird long-standing grudge against the company. Or maybe he's just got a bad case of writer's block. The point is, Julia, whatever is Mr. Potts's maniacal motivation, you and I are at a moral crossroads. Somebody has to stop this evil man."

"Whatever could be keeping Duane?" Julia whined,

looking around as if her boyfriend would emerge from the trees at any moment.

"Fine," I remarked, exasperated. "You stay here and scrounge for catfish and pokeberries the rest of your life. As for me, I'm off to save the world.

"C'mon, Jim," I added, as my trusty sable-colored sidekick stretched, yawned, and rose to his padded feet, still nursing his injured half a tail. "Let's go."

Morning at McDonald's

It's morning at McDonald's.

Bacon and sausage sizzling. Hotcakes on the griddle. Coffee, piping hot—but not too hot, not anymore, not since the lawsuit—and eggs cooking in perfect circles as if they were hamburger patties.

In the dining room, a mix of morning regulars. Two workmen wearing ball caps and T-shirts, one with a cell phone strapped to his belt, the other with long hair braided into a ponytail down his back. They've ordered the Deluxe Big Breakfast, with hotcakes, sausage, scrambled eggs, an oval of crisp plastic-tasting material called hash browns, and extra little tubs of maple-flavored corn syrup, packets of strawberry jelly, and paper thimbles containing ketchup from a community condiment-pumping station.

An old woman in a loose cotton housedress is dining alone on a bacon-and-cheese-and-egg biscuit. Two half-pints of low-fat milk in diminutive bottles sit at the edge of her paper placemat.

An old couple occupies a booth. He is quietly reading a complimentary copy of Monday's *Kansas City Star;* she is getting up to order him a refill for his coffee.

In the adjacent party room, dedicated to the once well known McDonald's advertising icon "Mac Tonight," a young mother with two small boys, one in a highchair, the other climbing over the back of his seat, tries to eat bites of fluffy pancake while talking on a cell phone. The phone is soon sticky with syrup.

A teenage girl has just driven up in a red Honda with a spoiler on the back. Another young woman is inside, settling down at a green-topped table with an Egg McMuffin, the first breakfast item ever offered by the chain, introduced, ironically, not far from here in Salina, Kansas, where McDonald's executives rightly presumed that if the product failed to catch on, no one would ever know.

In the corner, staring into a glass case, is a ten-year-old boy admiring this week's Happy Meal toys. They are Neopets—not the real ones that you feed and raise, but plush toy versions, like Beanie Babies, McDonald's biggest Happy Meal success.

On a carpeted stage rising twelve inches from the floor and protected by a brass rail, a life-size molded plastic Mac Tonight character is seated at a baby grand piano, emitting digitally programmed music turned low.

Dressed in a tailored black suit, knotted silver necktie, and black patent leather shoes, Mac Tonight looks like the famous singer Ray Charles, except that his head is china white and shaped like a crescent moon.

The music coming from the piano is an old Elton John tune called "Rocket Man" converted into a lilting piano solo. On the wall opposite is a neon sign as big as any Budweiser sign in any Hooters restaurant in the land, reading MAC TONIGHT.

Behind the counter and dispersed throughout the restaurant a crew of more than half a dozen workers in denim short-sleeve shirts and khaki trousers demonstrate the cleanliness and efficiency that have made McDonald's such an international sensation. The workers who aren't monitoring computerized cooking stations or taking drive-through orders via headphones are wiping tabletops, mopping floors, and restocking restrooms.

Except possibly for your branch library, no place in America could be calmer, more orderly, or more inviting than this particular McDonald's on this Monday morning.

And yet there is a yellow school bus crammed end to end with killer ferrets, like a joke shop's spring-loaded snakes in a can, on a highway somewhere in Arkansas, headed right this way.

The devious Daschell Potts, acknowledged genius, has abandoned his written plan to work his way along the Mississippi River, wreaking havoc here and there until arriving in Memphis for The Big One.

"That's just what they're expecting me to do," he told his meanest, snarliest ferret, Big Wolf. "But if they'd ever really understood my work, they'd know that I believe in the power of surprise."

Mr. Potts, of course, was referring to his literary masterpiece *Folderol,* in which every day the protagonist, an innocent fluffy duckling, encounters a completely unexpected hazard. An attack by a hungry chicken hawk. An alligator sleeping in an inlet. A safe falling from an airplane while the duckling is sleeping. A stick of dynamite left behind by a careless highway crew.

It's always something, Mr. Potts believed, and by always, he means always.

So into this peaceful picture in south Overland Park, Kansas, there is coming a brand of mayhem from which the world will not quickly recover.

How long before he strikes?

Much depends on the condition of the rented yellow school bus, and machinery, thank goodness, especially when few of its users take full responsibility for it, is not particularly reliable.

Twice already Mr. Potts has broken down, forced to seek help from incompetent, indifferent workers at Sinclair stations in tiny Arkansas towns.

Plus, ferrets, especially big ones, get hungry, so finding food enough for a bus full of them, even in a major chicken-raising state like Arkansas, was proving to be an ordeal for a solitary old man.

Soon he would have to find a place to spend the night. Few hotels welcome nonhuman guests. Fewer still welcome giant killer ferrets by the ton.

On a two-lane highway somewhere west of Little

Rock, Mr. Potts spies a billboard saying FREE CABLE TV, FREE CONTINENTAL BREAKFAST, PETS WELCOME, Y'ALL COME.

"Okay, boys," Mr. Potts announces. "We'll bivouac here."

The Collapsing Tunnel

While the dastardly Daschell Potts was piloting Weasel One down the Arkansas back roads in an effort to throw me off the giant ferrets' scent, Julia, Jim, and I remained castaways on Ferret Island.

As for the sudden appearance and disappearance of the interloping ex-congressman Pierre "Hercules" Narf, I had no idea where he was. He could have been a figment of my imagination. Heck, this whole story could be a figment of my imagination. I'm sure I would be the last to know.

Life does things to your mind.

For example, I know that I went on too long about not hearing trains, and how that brought on bouts of sleeplessness, and I confess, too, that I may not have connected that thought sufficiently with my conscious mind's failure to recognize that the "cave" was in fact a ferret-formed turnpike underneath the Mississippi River.

Forgive me. If these are flaws, they are flaws of narrative style, not of character. It is not my intention to tease the reader. So permit me to get right to the crux of the next problem: As amusing as ferrets can be, their engineering skills are inferior.

Let's face it.

Ferrets are no beavers.

They're not even as clever as people.

Jim and I splashed through the darkness toward whatever lay beyond.

Although we made progress, it was painfully slow, and I do mean painfully, as time and time again I stubbed my toes, smacked my elbows, and banged my head against unseen outcroppings.

Soon I was covered with bruises and soaked to the skin. Not only that, but I also suffered the olfactory discomfort of being in close proximity to a very wet weasel.

Gack! I gagged.

"If we ever get out of here alive, Jim," I advised, "I'm giving you a bath."

"*Chi-chi-chi,*" Jim replied, licking my hand.

From somewhere behind us came a dull rumbling

noise, like a train crossing a trestle over a high mountain pass, followed by the insistent hiss of a broken toilet.

"What th—?" I started to exclaim.

But before I could complete my reaction, a surge of chilly water struck, sweeping me through the darkness as the roof caved in.

Whether dug by machine, shovel, hand, or paw, tunnels under rivers spring leaks.

I wonder: If death is like sleep, do we dream? When we cross over to the other side of existence, do we still have thoughts from our childhood?

Snippets of holidays with our siblings. Remembrances of a carefree mom or dad. Ourselves, seen from afar, running in a field, or by the shores of a warm languid sea.

Scents. Sounds. Touches. Words.

Once death has claimed us, do we still fear being late for school, or unprepared for the exam, or being without clothes in front of the entire giggling class? Can our enemies still find us?

Once firmly established among the deceased, do we continue to imagine that we're falling through space? Or flying? Or crying?

I wonder if this is so.

Or are these alternating episodes of anxiety and gentle reassurance the proof that we need to know we're still alive, that while our conscious mind—tiny, weak, woefully unprepared—may have given up without a fight, our indefatigable subconscious remains committed to the case?

"Will," a voice was saying, "why are you so afraid of the world?"

It was my mother speaking; it was my doctor, my stepgrandmother, my kind sixth grade guidance counselor; it was the woman who sat beside me on the bus from St. Louis.

It was Julia.

She was holding a flashlight.

"Oh, Will," she cried. "Thank goodness. I was so afraid for you."

"What?" I asked, still unsure if I was dead or alive. "How did you find me?"

"I followed my nose," Julia answered. "Your ferret pal is—how shall I put it?—very ripe. Now hurry! The tunnel is collapsing!"

I squinted toward the weak pencil-thin beam of her flashlight.

"Which way?" I asked.

"I'm not sure," she answered, "but I know we can't stay here."

As if to prove her point, from somewhere within the cavern came another crash, followed by an echoing, reverberating boom. A stream of rushing water splashed across our feet.

Travels with Weasels

While tunnel walls were caving in all around us, with neither Julia nor I knowing the way to safety, if indeed there was a way, Daschell Potts, legendary author, winner of many of the world's most prestigious awards for literary achievement, and recently self-taught ringmaster of a traveling circus of giant killer ferrets, was negotiating with the night manager of a Ramada Inn somewhere near Conway, Arkansas, over the motel's pet policy.

"Your sign back there on the highway says 'Pets Welcome,'" a testy Mr. Potts said.

"I know what the dang signs says," the night manager replied. "I'm the one what nailed it up there. You think I can't read?"

"I don't know what your skills are, sir, nor do I care," Mr. Potts responded imperially. "I merely wish to confirm that there'll be no problem housing myself and my pets here for the night."

"Dogs or cats?" the night manager inquired.

"What difference does it make?" Mr. Potts asked. "You're not the one sleeping with them."

"Dogs cost more than cats," the night manager explained, "unless they're them little bitty dogs, the yappy kind, that just make little bitty messes, them are the same price as cats."

"So a very big dog would cost even more? Even more than, say, a goat, a monitor lizard, or a couple of boa constrictors?" Mr. Potts attempted to clarify.

"That's correct," the night manager continued. "If it's one of them Rootwilders, or Grape Dames, or big old flop-eared bloodhounds, then there is what is called a PP surcharge."

"'PP?'" Mr. Potts repeated.

"Poop premium," the night manager translated.

"Okay, now I'm beginning to understand," Mr. Potts said. "How much is it for the biggest dog on the list?

"That'd be an extra six bucks a night, on top of the regular room rate, the taxes, and the environmental disposal fee," the night manager quoted from memory.

"Is that per dog or for any number of dogs?" Mr. Potts asked.

"That, my friend, is the per-dog price," the night manager explained. "We base the price on what the animal is likely to produce while staying here."

"So if I had, say, fifty big dogs, let's call them part pit bull, part dachshund, and part English sheepdog, we could all stay here tonight so long as I'm willing to pay an extra three hundred dollars," Mr. Potts calculated.

"That's correct," the night manager said. "Although how you'd fit fifty Rootwilder-size mongrels into a motel room with one queen-size bed is a trick I'd like to see."

"Well, I'd have to charge you three hundred dollars to see a show as interesting as that," Mr. Potts advised the night manager. "Just one more thing."

"And what would that be?" the night manager said.

"Since my pets will be paying guests," Mr. Potts continued, "I assume they're entitled to the free continental breakfast mentioned on the sign back there on the highway."

"Hmmm," the night manager said. "I don't believe the question ever come up before. But if that's what the sign says, and I know it is, 'cause I nailed it up there myself, then I reckon you're right."

Using his Authors Guild MasterCard, Mr. Potts signed the register.

"Daschell Potts," the night manager said as he handed over the plastic card key to room 206, in the back, up the stairs, and to the right of the ice machine. "You ain't any relation to that guy what wrote *Folderol,* are you?"

"Possibly," Mr. Potts replied with great dignity. "I am not unfamiliar with the power of the written word."

"Woo-eee!" the night manager exclaimed. "That book changed my life. I absodutely-dab mean it! I first read *Folderol* so's I could pass sixth grade and was blown away with its big words and deep insights into my immortal soul. Wow, oh wow! Daschell Potts. *Folderol.* That dang book made me what I is today."

Mr. Potts grimaced uncomfortably.

"Look," the night manager said. "I don't have *Folderol* with me, but would you mind autographing a copy of *Backwater Motel Marketing*? It's the August issue. Brand new. I never even opened the cover, and that's the God's truth."

"My pleasure," Mr. Potts replied, performing the familiar request with the scribble of a ballpoint pen.

"Thanks a lot," the awestruck night manager said, staring at the scrawl on the slick magazine. "Enjoy your stay—and your complimentary breakfastses!"

Once each of his killers had been herded from the school bus into room 206, Daschell Potts tuned in to Animal Planet on the free cable TV and walked across the highway to McDonald's, where he placed a special order for fifty regular cheeseburgers, no mustard, no ketchup, no onions, plus a breaded chicken combo with a large Sprite Zero.

Alas, the moment he opened the motel room door with his armload of food, two of the ferrets, Bailey and Bogey, sprang outside and pounced on a pair of passing Yorkshire terriers, which they gobbled down as if they were broiled Cornish hens.

Mr. Potts shoved the errant ferrets back into the room and slammed the door.

All that remained of the Yorkies was a pair of little pink nylon leashes. These Mr. Potts took to the dumpster in the corner of the parking lot.

Dang! thought Mr. Potts. *If they get too much to eat on the road, they won't be hungry enough to do their work in Kansas City.*

Under the River

We were up to our necks in trouble.

The tunnel, once believed to be a cave, was coming apart. Daschell Potts was well on his way to committing ferret mayhem at some unsuspecting McDonald's. And Julia and I were as confused about our whereabouts as two fleas on a tap-dancing dog.

"What do you mean, you're not sure?" I said. "We just head in the opposite direction from where you came in. It's the first rule of tunnel travel. Enter at one end. Exit at the other. Right?"

"Well," Julia said, hesitating.

"Julia," I insisted. "It's a straight line. The shortest distance between two points. That's what a tunnel is!"

"Not *every* tunnel," Julia corrected me. "This was dug by ferrets, remember? You think they knew what they were doing? Nonsense. What we've got here is like a maze, with twisting passages, hidden rooms, and lots of dead ends."

"A maze!" I exploded. "Holy smokes! Who in their right mind would dig a maze of tunnels underneath a river?"

Once again, the aromatic Jim licked my hand.

"Their bodies may be big," Julia observed, "but their brains are regular ferret size."

Slogging through the muck on the cavern floor, trying to adjust my eyes to the bouncing beam, I asked Julia how she'd managed to get her hands on a flashlight.

"Oh, this?" she replied. "I found it at Mr. Potts's house. Under the circumstances, I didn't think he'd mind if I took it."

"I suppose not," I agreed.

We continued without speaking for a while, listening to the steady *ping* of water dripping around us, interrupted by the occasional distant *sploosh* of crumbling earth.

"So how did you learn that this is such a complex structure?" I asked, hoping to restart the conversation, adding, jokingly, "Did you read about it in the *Memphis Commercial Appeal*?"

The discovery of a system of tunnels beneath the

Mississippi River would make an excellent local newspaper story, I reasoned. It would be like stumbling from the jungles to discover the Panama Canal.

"Don't be silly, Will," Julia admonished. "Where would I get a newspaper? I learned about this place from a map."

More silence followed.

By now, I estimated, we were several hundred feet underground, trudging through a subterranean circulatory system designed by a lower life form led by impulse and happenstance. The air around us was about fifty-five degrees Fahrenheit. The water, lapping at our ankles, was chilly.

"Julia," I said. "Did I hear you correctly? Did you say something about a map?"

Like leaves stirred by an autumn breeze, a moldy locker room aroma wafted down the corridor, followed by the rich, primal scent of million-year-old earth.

Not speaking, Julia continued to splash ahead.

"Julia," I repeated. "Did you hear me? I asked you a question."

In the lead, Julia turned and shone the flashlight in my face.

"Okay, this is why I don't like to tell you things,"

she said accusingly. "Whenever I tell you something, you get mad."

"Excuse me?" I replied, not comprehending, but concluding the worst. "You mean, you found a map at Mr. Potts's house but you lost it?"

"Not exactly," she explained. "On the way to catch up with you, I decided to leave a note for Duane."

"And?" I said.

"And it was the only piece of paper I had," she said, as if that excused the foolishness of what she'd done.

"Oh, Julia," I lamented. "Has anybody ever told you that you have a problem with paperwork?"

"Whatever," Julia said dismissively. "I brought the flashlight, didn't I?"

When you're lost, time moves slowly.

I'm not saying that it seems to. I'm saying that's what it actually does. When you have no idea where you are, time literally slows down. Many people mistakenly assume that time is immutable, unchanging, like a car that's always traveling at exactly fifty miles an hour, or an oven that never deviates from its pre-set temperature of three hundred and fifty degrees. But such constants not only aren't the norm in nature; they are practically impossible to achieve.

Scientists have long known that time and space are

connected, that in some respects they're one and the same, two sides of the same theoretical coin. So it should come as no surprise to anybody that when you're lost, time comes close to standing still. Under these conditions, it moves at the speed of an ant crawling across a tablecloth through a blob of spilled honey.

Darkness slows time down, too. So does silence. So does fear. But these are scientific variables that I'll save for another discussion.

With the loyal Jim close behind us, Julia and I trudged through the watery sludge in the tunnel.

Where There's a Will, There's a Way

As interesting as the world is, there are times when it doesn't seem to work so well.

Two examples serve to illustrate my point.

The first, a complex of tunnels underneath the Mississippi River carved one toothy mouthful at a time by a team of very large ferrets.

The second, a broken-down yellow school bus parked at the Ramada Inn near Conway, Arkansas.

In each example, because someone failed to

perform a designated task correctly, others would suffer the consequences.

This fact is the foundation of the widespread belief among chronic complainers that life is unfair.

Previously carefree castaways on a sunny sandbar island, Julia and I were now within a minnow's sneeze of being buried and drowned within the same catastrophic instant. The tunnel was collapsing. The river was rushing in.

Meanwhile, a different sort of trouble had cropped up at the intersection of Interstate 40 and Arkansas Highway 65.

Wiping syrup from the stubble on his chin with a wadded-up paper napkin, having just finished a free continental breakfast for himself and fifty of his best-trained ferrets, the author turned urban terrorist Daschell Potts was unable to get his rented school bus started.

Rrrr, rrrr, rrrr, pop! it went whenever he turned the key.

"Dang, boys!" Mr. Potts cussed, giving the school bus a whack across its cracked and dusty dashboard. "Looks like we're stuck in Conway for a while."

Back inside the motel, Mr. Potts had to wait his turn

to arrange for a second night's stay. A woman standing in front of him was tearfully explaining to the desk clerk that her twin Yorkies had disappeared around dinnertime the night before.

"You'll still have to pay for their lodging, ma'am," the desk clerk explained. "Was they little dogs, you say? Then that'd be the same as two cats. Four dollars."

Mr. Potts stared innocently at the ceiling.

Two hundred miles away, inside the darkened tunnel, slogging along blindly while Julia held my hand, I stepped on a slippery channel catfish and instantly went down. For the second time in an hour, I found myself lying on my back in a rising tide of river water.

The more I experience life, the more I'm convinced that the critics were absolutely right: *Folderol* by Daschell Potts is the best book ever written.

Here's this solitary, defenseless duckling bobbing through the unknown at the mercy of every ripple on the water, every gust of wind, every twist of fate, an easy, appetizing source of protein for most of the animal species on the planet, resolutely continuing its journey despite a series of crushing setbacks.

And why?

Because even though the little waterfowl's heart is no bigger than an acorn, it's filled to overflowing with hope.

Hope.

It's what keeps us going when everything else is advising us to quit.

In his extraordinary wisdom, demonstrated before he became a dangerous weasel warrior, Mr. Potts had written, "Things always change. Sometimes they go from bad to good, sometimes from bad to worse. But this much is certain: Things always change."

And then—and this is what sets the legendary genius apart from today's merely popular writers—he adds this surprising addendum:

"Until the day arrives when everything is back to the way it was in the beginning."

Unknowingly, the duckling is swimming in a circle. If at any point along the way, for whatever reason, it decided to stop, to quit, to give up, well, obviously it would fail to achieve its destiny.

I'm no quitter.

Although far from home and deep beneath the collapsing earth, prone and bruised, with river water covering my ears, I held out hope that my situation would soon improve.

How can it not? I thought.

Where there is a Will, there is a way.

My old school motto.

Interestingly, sounds travel farther through water than they do through the atmosphere. It has something to do with the conductivity of the medium, the molecular density of water being more efficient at the transmittal of sound waves than the comparatively thin air.

Whales rely on this principle for long-distance communication, I've read, and everybody knows that whales are plenty smart.

So when I heard the warbled, washed-out voice of the Louisiana congressman Pierre "Hercules" Narf speaking as if he were calling through a tin-can telephone—"Quick! Grab him and toss him in the back"—I zeroed in on the direction from which the words had come and sat straight up.

"Come on, Julia," I announced manfully, still holding her hand. "We go this way!"

The Other Side

The voice of Congressman Narf transmitted through

the water was not a friendly one—indeed, something about his few short words portended greater danger—but at that moment it was a hopeful sound in that it suggested imminent rescue.

And after what Julia, Jim, and I had just been through, even a helping hand from Frankenstein's monster would have been accepted with gratitude.

But fate has so many tricks up her sleeve.

While I would dearly love to report that a couple of minutes later, Julia, Jim, and I emerged blinking into the bright southern sunlight, where we hitched a ride to Memphis with an affable traveling congressman and his coterie of amusing friends, ultimately to enjoy a tasty home-cooked meal at Nana's house, unfortunately, there was yet another unexpected hurdle to cross.

As I have said, the tunnel was quickly collapsing. Piece by piece, its ceiling was merging with its floor and its walls were closing inward, like elevator doors shutting for the final time. With each successive structural failure, water rushed in to obliterate the evidence.

It was a total engineering catastrophe, and Julia, Jim, and I, although only a few hundred yards from the exit, were a far cry from being out of the woods.

Natural caves hold countless dangers, among them narrowing passageways, blind alleys, and sudden, sharp dropoffs. Man-made tunnels are less of a problem, but without a map to go by, a navigator finds that they, too, are unpredictable.

Underground viaducts created by feral mustelids— giant wild ferrets—whose mandate from nature is to catch rats, rabbits, reptiles, and small birds, remain a mystery. This is an area of scientific research that has yet to attract sufficient funding. But take my word for it: Never hire ferrets to build anything for you.

To put the present dilemma into the proper perspective, there are a few cave-related facts worth reporting. In Croatia, to cite one example, explorers came across an underground pit with a direct vertical plunge of nearly 1,700 feet.

In the state of Georgia, the one in the former Soviet Union, not the one that squats like a hen atop Florida's panhandle, there's a cavern that's 5,600 feet beneath the ground.

The point is, when out for an afternoon of spelunking, watch your step.

Just when we thought we were going to be saved, Julia, Jim, and I fell into a hole that seemed as deep as the Grand Canyon. The only thing that kept us from being killed was that we fell onto an enormous pile of old, moldy innerspring mattresses. There must have been a thousand of the things. There were even a couple of Sleep Number beds with preset sleep numbers that proved to be perfect for landing on. As I recall, my ideal landing number is a six.

"Well," Julia sputtered, her head beneath her heels. "That's rural Arkansas for you. These people throw their trash just anywhere."

"I'm not sure I'd call this place just anywhere," I said in defense of a population I'd yet to meet. "There's a certain amount of thought that's gone into this."

"*Chi-chi-chi,*" added Jim.

"Have you noticed how he always takes your side?" Julia complained.

"He thinks you don't like him," I explained.

"In that case," she countered, "he's a much smarter weasel than most. Let's get to work."

By the time we'd piled up enough mattresses to build a sweeping, if unsteady, bouncy staircase to freedom and exited the tunnel where it terminated behind a pile of rusted-out Kenmore appliances and discarded Converse athletic shoes near a two-lane blacktop highway, Congressman Narf, if indeed that's whose garbled voice I'd heard underwater, was long gone.

So, it seems, was the tunnel.

Following an earth-shuddering rumble like a thousand well-fed wildebeest stampeding through a hard marble hall, the Mississippi River changed course, ceasing its primeval push downstream and diverting its massive captive energy into a vast swirling vortex, a colossal, bottomless whirlpool from which no vessel or fish or person could hope to escape.

It was as if the hand of Mother Nature herself, fumbling around for a great, cosmic, chrome-plated handle, had flushed the Father of Waters into oblivion.

Then, with a last lethargic *sploosh,* it was over. The water level bubbled back up to the banks, and the Mississippi River, refreshed, continued its journey to the sea.

"Talk about the nick of time," Julia observed.

"I'll say," I agreed.

Turnip Time

At sunrise, Julia and I caught a ride with an old man hauling produce in a pickup truck. He seemed a kind enough fellow, given that he stopped right away when we flagged him down. But initially he had a problem with Jim.

"Y'all ull hafta hitch th' pony to th' back," he said. "Got no room for livestock up here."

"He's not a—" Julia started to say.

"That's okay," I interrupted. "But we've come a long way and he's plenty tired. Is it okay if he just lies down in the back on your produce?"

The old man took off his hat and scratched his head. Then, while he was at it, he scratched his neck, his chest, and his sagging stomach through his soiled, stretched-out sleeveless V-neck undershirt.

"I reckon," the old man answered hesitatingly. "But he'll havta git down from there before we reach town. Nobody's gonna wanna buy a turnip that's been sat on by a Shetland pony."

"I see what you mean," I said agreeably, although to tell the truth, I didn't then and I'm not sure that I do now.

This aside, for much of the ride the old man turned out to be the ideal chauffeur. He didn't smoke, he didn't play the radio, and he didn't expect Julia and me to entertain him with breezy conversation. He just drove his battered pickup down that long empty highway as the sun came up and the rich black dirt of the Delta stretched all the way to the horizon as if it was the wine dark sea.

Meanwhile, as Julia and I motored to Memphis, Daschell Potts was still stuck in Conway, Arkansas, waiting for a bus part to arrive from a factory in rural China. The situation at the Ramada Inn was growing dire. Imagine, if you will, three days packed like salted olives into a single motel room with fifty giant ferrets becoming hungrier and meaner by the second.

WARNING: You may wish to skip this next part, as it contains a suggestion of terrible violence. In any event, although she'd been warned by the night manager not to, Maria Consuela "Britney" Lopez opened the door to room 206 to deliver clean sheets and two double rolls of itchy industrial-quality toilet paper. There was a brief scuffle, and then it was over. All that officials found later was her plastic nametag, somewhat larger than the standard tag, with tooth marks on it.

"Panthers," the sheriff concluded, shaking his head. "Endangered species, my hind end! They ought to shoot 'em all."

Meanwhile, Congressman Pierre "Hercules" Narf suddenly figured out that the tip Julia had given him about Mr. Potts traveling to Tuscaloosa, Alabama, was a ruse.

How?

It takes one to know one.

Slamming on his brakes in the middle of the road, Congressman Narf turned his pickup around and struck out for distant Conway, Arkansas, where he was part owner of the only garage in town and anxious to see one of his many far-flung girlfriends, this one a no-longer-young woman named Consuela who worked at the Ramada Inn.

Meanwhile again, I noticed a highway sign, bent into a kneeling position and riddled with rusty bullet holes, that said CONWAY—93 MILES.

"Where's Conway?" I asked, thinking that by now we should be getting pretty close to Memphis.

"Right where it's always been," the old man answered. "Smack dab in the middle of Arkansas."

"I thought we were in Mississippi," I said.

"Dunno why y'all 'ud think that," the old man replied. "This don't look nothin' like Mississippi."

"Yes, it does," Julia corrected. "It looks exactly like Mississippi. I ought to know."

"Maybe y'all oughta, but y'all don't," the old man said. "They's two 'tirely diff'rent places."

"I think you may be missing the point," I interjected politely. "It seems we're heading in the wrong direction."

"No, we ain't," the old man insisted. "I jest seen th' goll-durn sign. It says plain as day, 'Conway, ninety-three miles.' I kin read, cain't I?"

"Maybe we should get out up ahead," I suggested.

"Dang, if y'all ain't a coupla mind readers," the old man muttered.

He pulled over onto a farm road.

With the motor sputtering and threatening to quit at any moment, I hopped into the back of the pickup to retrieve Jim. But during the past few hours, the big bandy-legged weasel had become accustomed to gas-powered transportation. He didn't want to get out.

"Come on, Jim," I told him. "Ride's over."

Jim didn't budge.

"I mean it, Jim," I insisted, tugging on the loose layer of skin on his shoulders. "This is where we get off."

Jim shook his head, perhaps as a way of expressing "No," but equally effective at forcing me to let go. Caught off-guard, and thinking I was bracing myself, I shifted my foot from the steel lip of the truck bed onto the mountain of purple and white vegetables, each as round and unstable as a billiard ball.

Without so much as a "Hey, watch this!" I flipped over backwards, pitched through the air, and landed with a *whoomp* on the gravel, sending up a cloud of country dust that settled on my upturned face.

Interestingly, that was also when I saw that the old man's license plate read FITCH.

"Hey," I said. "Did you once live near the Mississippi River, like upstream, near Memphis?"

"I cain't think of why that'd be any bidness of yourn," he replied. "Now take your pony and git!"

The Road to Conway

I must confess that after falling off the turnip truck, I began to lose sight of a few essential details from my personal history. Perhaps it was the blow to the head. Perhaps it was something more cosmic than that. But if ever there was a fellow who had just fallen off a turnip truck, it was me, or I, depending on your level of achievement in the English language.

Why, for example, was I with this person, a nag-ging, hard-boiled, opinionated cutie pie named Julia, whose plans for life seemed to be dependent on the sudden, miraculous appearance of a dimwitted boyfriend named Duane?

Why was I in pursuit of the crazed literary genius Daschell Potts, whose goal in life involved unleashing carnivorous ferrets upon the innocent diners in roadside McDonald's restaurants?

Why didn't I just go back to my comfortable home in Kansas City and forget about the miserable experience of living on a worthless sandbar with native animals and getting up each day to fetch increasingly hard to find supplies for an ungrateful woman-child?

Now here I was, standing the middle of the highway, having been ejected from a beat-up pickup truck by a heavily weathered country bumpkin, some distance from the city of Conway, Arkansas, with no prospects, no plans, and, to my mind, no hope.

That was when Jim licked my hand.

Oh, Jim, I thought, nuzzling his pointy, ferret-smelling face. *You're such a good guy. Am I ever glad that I found you.*

"You're kissing the ferret?" Julia exclaimed. "What, you don't think that I find you weird enough already?"

"Jim and I have been through a lot together," I explained.

"Yeah," Julia responded. "So have my shower drain and I. You think that gives me license to lick it? Holy smokes, Will! Get a life!"

Perhaps sudden insights are common on the road to adventure, but at that humiliating moment I saw clearly that Julia and I were not destined to have a long and fruitful future together.

Our "friendship," such as it was, had been a confluence of circumstance. We were two meandering tributaries joined by sheer chance to form a meager shallow stream, only to be diverted once again by the first impediment to be placed in our path—or possibly the sixth or seventh, depending on how you tabulate a sequence of unsafe boats, wide rivers, crazy authors, giant ferrets, collapsing tunnels, goofy farmers, and a spate of exceptionally bad luck.

I did just fall off a turnip truck, I realized.

It amazes me how ignorant I am. You name it, I don't know it: How things work. Why things happen. What causes what. I'm a little yellow duckling paddling in a big wide circle, thinking that I'm on some pioneering adventure, nearing some huge, rewarding goal.

The truth is, I barely get C's in Spanish, am way over my head in algebra, can't hold on to a football, am clueless about how to dress, and don't even know how to dance.

Then, just as I was succumbing to self-pity, wallowing like a pig in the slough of despond, wondering if I'd ever be able to figure out anything in time for it to matter, the resplendent truth of Daschell Potts's classic novel *Folderol* dazzled me once again.

"There are no accidents," he'd written in chapter six, referring specifically to the tragic scene in which the duckling is struck by a superheated meteorite, from which he recovers only in time to be clobbered by a falling safe, a boulder, a series of increasingly heavy lead weights, a cement truck, and an errant baby grand piano—a mahogany Fritz Gerber & Sons.

"Whatever happens," he went on, "happens in order to connect you to what happens next, which is your destiny."

What an extraordinary expression of faith!

And what extraordinary proof now followed.

The dense, towering topiary of frog green kudzu vine that lined the Arkansas highway and cascaded haphazardly from the leaning creosote poles and sagging power lines framed a fast-moving cloud of dust, an apparition that quickly parted to present a bright red tricked-out Pontiac Grand Prix headed in my direction. Just before it reached me, the customized automobile spun to a stop in the gravel and the door on the driver's side opened.

"Hey!" a woman's voice called out. "Don't I know you?"

Incredibly, it was none other than Miss Foster, the woman who'd shared her zucchini bread with me on the bus to Memphis so many weeks ago.

What a strange coincidence! I thought.

"Why don't you and your weasel get out of the road, goofball," Julia suggested. "Or haven't you had enough trouble?"

Miss Foster's Wild Ride

"Hello," I greeted Miss Foster. "How's your grandfather, the junk food wrapper genius?"

"The Happy Meal inventor? That was my great-uncle," she corrected me. "And he's still dead."

"Oh," I replied, embarrassed, recalling too late that when we first met, Miss Foster had been en route to her great-uncle's funeral in Yazoo City, Mississippi.

"That's okay," she assured me. "It was his time. He was nearly one hundred and four years old."

"*Whew!*" I responded. "That's quite an achievement. What was his secret?"

"Showing up," she replied. "He always said it's the secret to success."

Hmmm, I thought. *I'll bet he wishes he'd skipped the funeral.*

As I was soon to learn, the flashy performance car Miss Foster was driving had been a deathbed gift from her great-uncle. It's too bad that the old fellow hadn't been driving a Yukon or an Escalade when he expired, because Julia and I had to squeeze together to share a seat in the front, while Jim was folded up like a switchblade knife in the back.

"Lord, that's a big dog," Miss Foster said, once we were under way. "Does it eat a lot?"

"Depends on how you cook," Julia answered. "He likes things spicy."

"So I noticed," Miss Foster replied with a wave of her fingertips beneath her nostrils. "Whoo-ee, doggie, *Stink City!*"

(In using this expression, Miss Foster was aware that she was providing a not-so-subtle plug for another highly entertaining novel by the author of *Ferret Island*.)

As it turned out, Miss Foster was driving to Little

Rock, Arkansas, to pick up a marker for her great-uncle's grave.

"I'd appreciate it if you kids could help me load it into the car," Miss Foster said. "I imagine it's quite heavy. My great-uncle wrote instructions for what it should say, but after listing his achievements—the Happy Meal, the Bloviated Hairdresser, and the Tchotche Museum—by the time you add the literary passage it gets a trifle long."

"Oh?" I responded. "What did he choose?"

"'Peculiar travel suggestions are dancing lessons from God,'" she quoted.

"What?" Julia said, wrinkling her nose.

"It's by Daschell Potts," I explained. "It's the famous last sentence in *Folderol,* although some sore-heads claim that Mr. Potts plagiarized it from a guy named Kurt Vonnegut."

"That's right," Miss Foster said. "So you've read *Folderol?*"

"Many times," I told her, flinching as she blasted through a red light in Hooterville.

"Interesting man, Daschell Potts," Miss Foster observed.

"If you say so," Julia countered, the two of us cinched together in the front seat belt like pillows in a "buy one get one free" pack at Wal-Mart.

"Is that a gun?" I asked, spying a sidearm strapped to Miss Foster's calf.

"Oops," Miss Foster said, abruptly changing lanes in front of a moving van on I-530. "I guess the cat's out of the bag."

"Cat?" I repeated.

"Bag?" Julia added.

"*Chi-chi-chi,*" chimed in Jim.

"Special Agent, part-time, Emily Foster, FBI," Miss Foster announced, using an official-sounding voice and extending her hand in greeting, at seventy-five miles an hour an ill-advised gesture that caused the Grand Prix to swerve from the roadway onto the shoulder.

"I thought you were a dance instructor," I said, gripping the dashboard.

"That, too," Miss Foster confirmed. "Ballet. Waltz. Tango. Hip-hop. Chicken dance. But I also do piece-work for the United States Department of Justice. After I deliver the stone, I'm back on the trail of a suspected terrorist. Interestingly, it's the man we were just talking about—Daschell Potts."

"Incredible," I said. "What a small world."

"No kidding," my seat-belt buddy added, her lips

159

grazing my ear in a manner that under other circumstances I might have taken as affection. "That sandbar was bigger."

Miss Foster jammed on the brakes and skidded in a semicircle around an armadillo ambling across the highway.

"Is there much training involved in your job?" Julia asked, gripping the door handle as Miss Foster stomped on the accelerator.

"What?" Miss Foster shouted above the roar of the three-hundred-and-twenty-horsepower engine.

"What makes you suspect Mr. Potts?" I asked.

"A tip," Miss Foster replied.

"Let me guess," Julia said. "It was some creepy ex-congressman, right?"

"Our sources are confidential," Miss Foster declared. "But how did you know it was Narf?"

Julia gazed out the side window and shook her head in disbelief.

"If this world gets any smaller," she muttered, "you'll be able to Scotch-tape it to my Grandma Doogan's brooch."

"Doogan?" Miss Foster responded in surprise. "My mother's name was Doogan. Where are you from?"

Unfortunately, the search for a common ancestor

would have to wait, as a highway sign advised us that Miss Foster had overshot Little Rock and was now skidding into Conway, Arkansas, where as destiny would have it, many paths were about to cross once again.

As Miss Foster pulled into the parking lot of the Cracker Barrel restaurant, I asked, "Does anybody else have to go to the bathroom?"

Lunch Break in Conway

If McDonald's is where hometown America gets a burger and saves a buck, the Cracker Barrel is where traveling America can count on adding a happy pound or two just from the gravy.

This is a friendly, wholesome, visually entertaining place based on big servings of fried food and slabs of sweet pie, the roadside diner as it was meant to be, complete with postcards, Beanie Babies, souvenir T-shirts, and, if you shop carefully, the occasional whoopee cushion.

What's not to like about the Cracker Barrel?

After washing my hands in the Conway, Arkansas's Cracker Barrel's near-spotless restroom, I joined Miss

Foster and Julia at a plastic-topped table where a college student named Chad was distributing plastic glasses of iced tea with fat wedges of discolored lemon.

"So," I said. "How far are we from the tombstone factory?"

Miss Foster wrinkled her face.

"Quite a ways, I'm afraid," she answered. "It's back down the highway in Little Rock."

"The meatloaf looks good," Julia observed.

"I was thinking maybe the chicken and dumplings," I replied.

While Miss Foster continued to study the menu, I studied the room. It seemed to be sort of an RV crowd, with a handful of locals thrown in.

The most obvious feature of the clientele was that except for Julia and me, and possibly Chad, there were no other kids. Just about everybody had hair that was in the process of turning a different color, like the deciduous leaves of autumn.

Next door was a busy McDonald's, where minivans and SUVs were lined up at the drive-through. Across the street was a Ramada Inn with a sheriff's cruiser parked in the unloading zone and, on the side near the back, a yellow school bus with its front end jacked up. A man was lying on his back underneath, apparently working on the engine.

"Tell me about your search for Daschell Potts," I asked Miss Foster. "What clues have you got to go on?"

Miss Foster looked up from the menu at the hovering Chad, pencil in hand.

"How's the country fried steak today?" she asked.

"It's our most popular dish," Chad replied, as if he were a robotic installation at a theme park.

"I'll have that," she said, "with extra biscuits and sausage gravy."

"You bet," said Chad, scurrying away.

"You were asking?" Miss Foster said.

"The Daschell Potts case," I repeated. "What have you got to go on?"

As I spoke, Jim, my trusted giant ferret and close companion, locked inside Miss Foster's Pontiac Grand Prix, was scratching at the window. Either he was hungry or he needed to go to the bathroom.

"The key to finding Potts," Miss Foster announced, adding unnecessarily, "—and you do realize that this information is top secret—is to locate a flock of giant parrots. We have a tip that Potts is planning to unleash them on the world."

"Parrots?" repeated Julia. "Are you sure you've got that right?"

"That's the information our source has provided us," Miss Foster replied. "And he's been on the scene."

"Giant parrots," I said, as Chad placed steaming hot plates around the table. "Not carrots, or lariats, or, oh, I don't know, possibly ferrets?"

"Nope," Miss Foster insisted. "It was definitely parrots. I took the call myself."

"Interesting," I said.

Suddenly, on the other side of the restaurant, in an adjoining room, hidden behind an alcove and squeezed into the back of a secluded booth, Congressman Pierre "Hercules" Narf came into my view, dining on a whole catfish supper, with deep-fried hush puppies, curly fries, coleslaw, and a double slice of lemon meringue pie.

He did not appear to have seen us.

"Julia," I whispered, trying to signal her without Miss Foster taking notice. "Arf-nay is ear-hay."

"Don't bark at me, buster," Julia said, making a deep crater in her mountain of mashed potatoes so it would retain more gravy. "I'm getting pretty tired of you ordering me around."

"You don't understand," I said.

"I've been researching these giant parrots and have concluded that the only way Potts could obtain them is from a disgruntled former breeder for the Rainforest Café in Kansas City," Miss Foster continued. "So, once I've placed my great-uncle's grave marker, I'm going to Kansas City to check things out."

"Is this a fairly typical government plan?" Julia asked. "Or did you just make it up all on your own?"

"This is your federal government at work," Miss Foster replied. "I have supervisors appointed by the president himself. I'm hardly what you'd call a loose cannon. Did you know that parrots are related to dinosaurs? Think about what would happen if dinosaurs were roaming our cities."

"Incredible," Julia said, as, through the Cracker Barrel window, I watched Jim shredding the Grand Prix's upholstery.

"You know, I think my dog needs a walk," I announced, pushing my plate aside. "Order me the blackberry pie. I'll be right back."

Holy smokes, I thought, once outside with Jim, relieving himself on a bush. *If anybody is going to stop Mr. Potts from unleashing his ferrets, it's me.*

The fate of the civilized world is in my hands.

A Whiff of Trouble

Jim and I were standing outside the Cracker Barrel in Conway wondering why there were so many empty rocking chairs on the restaurant's porch when I detected a familiar foul stench in the air.

At first, quite reasonably, I assumed that it had something to do with Jim's having just peed on a near-dead holly bush at the edge of the parking lot, but this odor was no mere splash of *eau de polecat*. This aroma permeated the atmosphere as if a circus wagon filled with performing weasels were passing by, one that's been on the road for many weeks without the mandatory hosing down.

Lordy! I thought. *Does Conway always smell like this? No wonder these people have a tourism prob-lem!*

Just then, Julia stepped through the front doors of the restaurant carrying a small triangular Styrofoam box.

"Here," she said. "We got tired of waiting."

"Where's Miss Foster?" I asked.

"She's paying the bill," Julia explained. "She said for us not to worry because it's official government business. Anyhow, she's in the gift shop looking for novelty nightlights, something that she collects and is accustomed to putting on her expense account."

"Corruption seeks the lowest level," I observed. "It's the trickle-down theory."

"Whatever," Julia replied. "Here's your pie."

"Yum," I replied.

But I wasn't quick enough. Jim, who had been confined to Miss Foster's car for hours, snatched the package and gobbled it down in a single gulp, Styrofoam and all.

"Dang, it stinks out here," Julia said. "What is it with this place?"

"I think it's coming from across the street," I told her. "From behind the motel."

"Well, that's got to be good for business," Julia replied sarcastically, adding, "You know, we're no more than four hours from Marmaduke, so I thought I'd go over to the Ramada Inn and call Duane to pick me up and take me home. Not that I'm bailing out on you, Will, but enough's enough. You understand."

"Of course," I replied, strangely disappointed. "In

fact, I was planning to go over there myself. I assume Miss Foster is going to Little Rock. I've got to find a way to get to Memphis to stop Mr. Potts."

"Miss Foster is off on a wild parrot chase," Julia confirmed. "I tried to convince her that maybe she'd misunderstood what the tipster had said, but she just laughed and said, 'You silly girl. How could giant clarinets threaten our nation's security?' So I figured, Okay lady, have it your way. I'm outta here."

"You're a sensible girl, Julia," I said sincerely. "I'll never forget you."

"Likewise," she told me. "It's been a hoot."

Together, we dashed across the highway with Jim at our heels. The moment we walked into the lobby of the Ramada Inn, the desk clerk said, "We charge a premium for dogs, and big dogs are assessed with the biggest premium—six dollars."

"Seems fair," I replied.

"What kind of dog is that, if I may ask?" the desk clerk inquired.

"Well, let me see," I said, "he's half dachshund, half Great Pyrenees, half alligator, and half Tasmanian skunk."

"That's four halves," the desk clerk observed, frowning, as if he were an eighth grade math teacher and I were the classroom dunce. "In which case, it'll be twelve dollars extra."

"You drive a hard bargain," I said, "but you have us over a barrel. We need two singles for the night. One with a dog, one without. Both near the ice machine, if possible."

"Not a problem," the desk clerk replied. "I just happen to have one checking out, and the other will be available as soon as the guest gets back from a double pet funeral. You're welcome to wait in the self-serve laundry while the substitute maid readies the rooms."

"Substitute maid?" I asked. "What happened to the regular maid?"

"If I told you, you wouldn't want the room," the desk clerk replied.

"I'm sure there's a lot about this place I'd rather not know," Julia observed. "Thanks for your sensitivity."

"Sign here," the desk clerk instructed, pushing registration cards to Julia and me.

"What do I put down as my business?" I whispered to Julia, finding the questions on the card to be downright nosy.

"Try wildlife trapper," Julia suggested. "It's close enough."

"Thanks," I said. "What are you putting down?"

"Victim," she whispered. "But don't worry. I'm not mentioning your name."

We turned in our cards, received our electronic keys, and strolled to the heated indoor swimming pool to wait until our rooms were ready. The enclosure was quite steamy and smelled strongly of chlorine gas. Because of the steam the windows were completely clouded. I walked around to the shallow end of the pool and wiped a circle in the window with my sleeve. What I saw in the parking lot astonished me so much that I stumbled backwards and fell into the water.

"*Yi!*" I cried.

I had not imagined it.

With the engine running, Daschell Potts was stuffing the last of his giant ferrets into a yellow school bus.

A Posse of Two

"For goodness' sake, Will," Julia cried, as I spit out water from the overchlorinated pool. "Couldn't you wait until you got to your room to take a bath?"

"It's Mr. Potts," I sputtered.

"Well, of course it's hot," she said. "You're in the hot tub."

"No," I insisted, standing up and shaking water from my clothes. "I'm talking about outside, getting into a yellow school bus with his gang of giant ferrets. Mr. Potts is not in Memphis. He's here!"

Julia peered through the porthole I'd wiped in the window.

"Not for long," she observed. "It's pulling onto the highway right now."

"We've got to stop him!" I cried.

Julia tossed me a terrycloth towel from a nearby rack.

"Sit down, Will," Julia ordered. "We have to talk."

"But he's getting away!" I cried.

"Listen, Will," she said in her most serious voice, "this has been amusing, but it's not for me. Chasing after washed-up, addled-brained, partially pickled writers who're heavily armed with killer weasels is what you do. It's not what I do. I'm going home, okay? Duane will pick me up in the morning, and tomorrow night I'll be sleeping in my own white-painted sleigh bed in Marmaduke."

"But Mr. Potts plans to kill people," I pleaded. "Surely that matters."

"Of course it matters," Julia agreed, "and that's why fate chose you to stop him. I was merely along for the ride."

"But—" I started to protest once again.

"I'll give you my address," she continued. "I'll even watch after Jim for a few days. But I'm not going with you. By the way, that school bus is not on its way to Memphis. When the stinkmobile pulled onto the highway, it was headed west on Highway Forty, toward Fort Smith, Arkansas."

Although I was still dripping wet, Julia put her arms around me and hugged me tightly. Then, almost as an afterthought, she kissed me on the mouth for what seemed like forever.

"Take care of yourself, kiddo," she said softly.

"Y'all's rooms is ready," the substitute maid announced. Her nametag identified her as Marcia Powell, Mayor of Conway, leading me to suspect that neither job paid very well.

"I doused the one room with a whole jug of Pine-Sol," Mayor Powell announced, "so it should be okay—leastwise, I hope it is."

"We'll put the dog in that one," Julia said. "I'm sure it'll be fine."

I still faced a number of hurdles. Dry clothes, for one. Transportation to follow the yellow school bus, for another. Since I was too young for a driver's license, renting a car was out of the question. That left riding the Greyhound or hitchhiking, neither of which I would recommend for anyone.

As I have observed many times, fate has a way of taking over when you least expect it. In this case, destiny took the form of a scowling, red-faced, middle-aged, and beer-gutted congressman, Pierre "Hercules" Narf, who suddenly appeared in the Ramada Inn swimming enclosure dressed only in a tight black Speedo.

The sight was so disturbing that Julia gasped and Mayor Powell fainted dead away.

"Oh," Congressman Narf observed. "So it's you kids. Why am I not surprised?"

"Your Excellency," I replied. "How nice to see you again."

"Not likewise, I'm sure," he said, diving into the deep end and beginning a series of laps, during which time Julia revived Mayor Powell and escorted her and Jim out of the area. Just as the glass door closed behind her, Julia turned and gave me a last little wave with her fingers.

My heart felt strangely pained.

Such a pretty girl!

After ten minutes of back-and-forth swimming, the disagreeable Congressman Narf climbed out of the pool, plopped himself into a rubber-strapped chair, which strained beneath his weight, and dried his carbuncular face with a hotel towel.

"So what gives, kid?" he asked. "Tell me what you know."

"I take it that you're referring to Mr. Potts?" I responded.

"I'm not talking high school algebra," he replied. "Spill it or I spill you."

"He's headed up Highway Forty toward Fort Smith," I replied. "After that, I don't know."

"Son of a gun has pulled a fast one," Congressman Narf observed. "But that's okay. We'll get him."

"What's your interest in Mr. Potts?" I inquired. "I thought you were in jail."

"I was," he answered. "But now I'm on special assignment for the United States Department of Homeland Security."

"They recruit people from prison?" I asked.

"It's a good training ground for government work," he explained.

"Interesting," I said.

"Business is business," Congressman Narf recited. "And so is politics."

"May I join you in the chase?" I asked. "I have a personal stake in this."

"Why now?" he replied. "I could use a bagman."

"A bagman?" I repeated, not understanding the term.

"A gopher. A grunt. A minion to fetch coffee and doughnuts. That sort of thing," he explained.

"What's it pay?" I asked, inspired to play hardball with this guy.

"Something less than cleaning rooms at the Ramada Inn in Conway, Arkansas," he answered. "So are you in?"

"I'm in," I said, without thinking.

But of course I should have thought.

Closing In on a Maniac

By the time Congressman Narf had changed into more presentable clothes and I had managed to locate some dry duds as well, Mr. Potts and his bus full of bloodthirsty ferrets had gained a substantial head start.

"How do you expect to catch up with him in this?" I asked Congressman Narf, whose rusty vehicle, a sputtering, backfiring Datsun pickup truck, obviously had seen better days, and possibly better countries.

"Are you kidding me?" he replied. "This is exactly what we need for capturing that crackpot."

"How do you figure?" I asked, always willing to learn from my elders.

"Well, criminy," Congressman Narf responded, in that "kids are so stupid" voice that adults too often employ. "Look at what the fool is driving! If he were hauling helium balloons he'd get maybe ten miles to the gallon, and that lunatic has stuffed his bus full of fifty ferrets as fat as bull walruses. I figure he'll be stopping to refuel about every twenty minutes. Don't worry. We'll catch him."

Half an hour later, we pulled into Tim's Diesel, Gas, Showers, and Snacks just outside Russellville, Arkansas, to ask questions. To my horror, there was no one around to ask questions of. The snacks had been ransacked, the diesel pump was still running, and all that remained of Tim was a pair of Tony

Lama boots standing upright behind the cash register.

"Potts," pronounced Congressman Narf gravely. "His rampage has begun."

Back in the Datsun, Congressman Narf pushed the accelerator all the way to the floor and the speedometer slowly climbed to thirty-five.

"We're getting close," he announced. "Those boots were still warm."

"Question," I said.

"Yeah, what?" he replied.

"Well, if you're with the government and you're after Mr. Potts, and Miss Foster is with the government and she's after Mr. Potts, why are you two hundreds of miles apart, heading in different directions?"

"Because my department doesn't talk to her department," he explained.

"And why is that?" I asked.

"A long time ago her boss and my boss were up for the same job in Washington. Her boss got it. My boss was transferred to Doniphan County, Kansas, to be a school crossing guard," Congressman Narf said. "You gotta understand, kid, in this world, everything is politics."

I thought about the life lessons revealed in Daschell Potts's classic work, *Folderol.* In that elegant allegory, the duckling learns to get by on his own resources and optimism. He doesn't form fragile alliances that can be broken.

This thought brought to mind my recent partnership with the winsome Julia.

My heart became heavy once again.

"Here's a Conoco," Congressman Narf announced. "Let's check it out."

If anything, the scene at the Conoco was worse than the mayhem at Tim's. Diesel pump left running, snack foods scattered and torn open, and a pair of deflated Air Jordans halfway out the door, still steaming from body heat.

"This looks really bad," I said.

"I'm guessing he's gonna turn right at the Oklahoma border," Congressman Narf announced.

"How do you figure that?" I asked.

"Are you pulling my leg or what?" Congressman Narf snapped back impatiently. "Who in his right mind would go to Oklahoma?"

"Mr. Potts is not in his right mind," I reminded him. "You said so yourself."

"I never said he was *that* crazy," Congressman Narf countered. "Anyway, I trust my instincts."

"So what's his destination, then?" I pressed, if this

wiseacre was so all-fired smart about everything.

"One of two places," Congressman Narf proposed. "Either he's headed for the headquarters of Wal-Mart in Bentonville, Arkansas, where he could make a real name for himself by setting a few ferrets loose on the fashion buyers, or he's going to Kansas City."

"Why Kansas City?" I asked, mindful that it was my home and that, like the duckling in *Folderol,* if I got there, I would have made a complete circle around the pond, so to speak.

"This is the last question I'm gonna answer," Congressman Narf insisted. "After that, you don't speak until spoken to, get it?"

"Okay," I agreed.

"He's going to Kansas City," Congressman Narf declared, "because they've got some crazy little women there and he's going to get him one."

Nonsense, I thought.

The once great Daschell Potts was going to Kansas City to terrorize the innocent customers of McDonald's. Something about the place had caused his aged mind to snap. I don't know what it was or when it happened, but something had caused Mr. Potts to go from being the world's greatest writer to being the world's most extreme food critic.

It made no sense to me. Especially since McDonald's has begun selling premium coffee, crispy salads with balsamic vinaigrette dressing, and cooked-to-perfection broiled chicken sandwiches. I mean, it's not as if they're forcing you to order the supersize fries.

But if you do, they're happy to give you extra ketchup.

Yum!

Natural-Born Killers and Shoplifters

Inside the yellow school bus, Daschell Potts was losing control.

It was designed to seat up to sixty-five reasonably well-behaved children who, when you average the fat ones and the skinny ones and the short ones and the tall ones, could be considered of normal size, and his passengers consisted of fifty nasty bloated ferrets, some of whom had blood on their faces and all of whom were covered with a fine layer of Cheese Doodle powder, as if they were orange mine workers headed home after a hard day underground.

And neither were they sitting still like schoolchildren are expected to do. Instead of satiating their appetites, the recent raids on the roadside fueling stations had worked them into a cheese-dust-and-sugar frenzy.

Hoping to calm them down, Mr. Potts had put a Ray Charles CD on the bus's PA system. His idea backfired. No sooner did the melodious strains of "Here We Go Again" begin than the ferrets, predisposed to physical outbursts, began dancing atop the cracked leather seats and up and down the narrow, candy wrapper–littered aisle. The school bus, a top-heavy contraption if ever there was one, began to heave and haw like a sailboat in a squall.

Mr. Potts was beside himself. Things were not proceeding smoothly. For one, it was not out of cunning that he taken the longer, meandering Arkansas route, as he had once tried to convince himself. He had taken it because he made a wrong turn and missed the main highway to Memphis.

For another, he had no idea that while living on the sandbar the price of fuel had shot up to three dollars a gallon. How had that happened? Was no one running the country anymore? Every time he filled the tank, it cost Mr. Potts one hundred and eighty dollars, and he was already near empty again.

The map he was using was so covered with fine orange-colored particles that he could make out only the large type, and the large type was limited to the big cities. As near as he could tell, the next big city was Kansas City.

Oh, well, he sighed. *One McDonald's is pretty much the same as another.*

But of course, we know that this is not true. In Overland Park, Kansas City's biggest and beigest suburb, there is a unique McDonald's that celebrates the momentary celebrity of Mac Tonight, a moon-headed character who looks like Ray Charles.

Now, I don't want some nitpicky reader sending an e-mail to the publishing company saying, "But I thought that's where he was planning to go all along. Didn't you suggest as much in a whole chapter earlier on?"

Let me remind you that this is Daschell Potts we're talking about. A man who spent countless years hidden on a faux island in the middle of the Mississippi, typing plans for all sorts of mayhem in every little hamlet between Jackson, Mississippi, and Memphis, Tennessee. A hermit, a heavy drinker, a has-been, an artist. His plans were no more substantial than a single strand of gossamer thread spun by a common garden spider. His eyesight was poor, his knees creaked, his back hurt, his teeth needed attention, his brain was awash in whiskey, and one ear was missing, and you object because you detect no consistency in his plans?

You must be an academic, Mr. or Mrs. or Miss or Ms. E-mailer. I suggest you get out into the real world more often.

Meanwhile, back to Mr. Potts. He'd pulled into a Sinclair station ten miles south of Fayetteville, Arkansas, to get diesel fuel, and, of course, all the ferrets came spilling out like circus clowns from a trick car. While Mr. Potts filled the cavernous tank, the ferrets ripped open packages of stale Ding-Dongs and dispatched the clerk, a stout woman in her fifties, employing a sudden and ghastly double gulp, leaving behind only the unfortunate woman's pink flip-flops.

The situation, Mr. Potts observed, was getting serious. As he put the latest fuel charge on his Author's Guild MasterCard, he saw that it was now dangerously close to exceeding the preset limit.

Murder by ferret is one thing.

Bad credit is quite another.

In Fayetteville, traffic had slowed to a crawl, with most of the roads clogged with buses just like Mr.

Potts's Weaselmobile. It was football weekend at the University of Arkansas, and through an astonishing series of unlikely events the Razorbacks remained undefeated. Nearly all of Arkansas was there, including the ubiquitous Mrs. Clinton, who, to tell the truth, had never cared much for Arkansas in the first place. She preferred big cities.

While Mr. Potts fussed and fumed and honked his horn, he should have been expressing his gratitude, for with so many yellow buses attempting without success to move in every direction, Mr. Potts could not be singled out by the scowling man and the fresh-faced boy in the beat-up Datsun pickup truck just six car lengths behind him.

Congressman Narf, apparently having been through such episodes many times before, simply reclined his seat, rolled down his window, lit a cigarette, and turned on the radio.

A Ray Charles tune was playing.

It was "Making Believe."

Kansas City, Here We Come

It is hard to know whether the acceleration of life's

184

coincidences have evolved over time, or whether they are mounting evidence of intelligent design, but whichever the case, there is no denying that we are living in an age of relentless coincidence.

Consider this pertinent example: In the bustling modern city of Overland Park, Kansas, there are two full-time police officers assigned to animal control duty.

For the most part, their job consists of scooping up flattened squirrels, skunks, and possums, rounding up runaway dogs and cats, responding to complaining neighbors about the sound of barking, and, on certain rare occasions, removing a recently deceased deer or split-shelled armadillo from the centerline of a cross street.

Sometimes they answer calls from hysterical widow women who discover an owl in the bedroom, but not usually. Basically, for an animal control officer, it's a quiet life, marked with poignant daily reminders of how briefly burns life's candle.

One of the two animal control officers was a woman well into middle age by the name of Taffy Malone. Now here is the astonishing coincidence:

In 1957, the then ten-year-old Taffy Malone was living with her mother and father in Kennett,

Missouri, when, in the middle of the night, the spring floods rose up and carried their farmhouse out into the Mississippi River, including Taffy Malone's two pet ferrets, Snowball and Louise, who, though terrified, clung tenaciously to a wooden kitchen table until they were deposited gently by fate on a sandbar somewhere south of Memphis.

From this cataclysmic, almost biblical beginning arose the race of giant ferrets that were now under the demonic dominion of Daschell Potts, the most dangerous fifty of which were now traveling north with him on Highway 71 toward Taffy Malone's new townhouse, which faced a golf course and goose preserve in idyllic south Overland Park.

Of course, once you begin such a line of inquiry, you quickly discover that coincidences are as plentiful as the stars that sparkle in God's scattered galaxies.

Taffy Malone had just finished unsticking a particularly adhesive groundhog from a busy intersection when it occurred to her that she should wash her hands.

Now, who has the cleanest bathrooms in town? No, it's not any of the country clubs. All they're good for is a free pocket comb, a small terrycloth towel, and maybe a swig or two of mint-flavored mouthwash.

No, the answer, not surprisingly, is McDonald's. With the occasional rare exception of the part-time help, everything about McDonald's is squeaky clean. So that's where Taffy Malone was headed after pulling the two-dimensional groundhog from the road, and, coincidence or not, the closest McDonald's at that moment was the very McDonald's dedicated to the fleeting fame of Mac Tonight.

"I suppose I'll wash up and get myself a burger," Taffy Malone announced to the cadavers in the back of her truck, which she parked in front of a nearby and now closed bank. "You guys stay put."

Meanwhile, Daschell Potts was having trouble figuring out which highway to take out of Harrisonville, Missouri. It was all so confusing, and the ferrets weren't helping one bit. Still dancing to Ray Charles tunes, in this case, "Hit the Road, Jack," they nearly tipped the school bus over onto a passing SUV, which, coincidentally, was being driven by a gossip columnist for the *Kansas City Star* named Hearne Christopher, Jr., who would come to regret not having stopped the bus to interview so famous a celebrity as Daschell Potts.

Congressman Narf and I were right on Mr. Potts's tail. This wasn't easy, because the top speed of the congressman's car was some five miles per hour less than the minimum speed permitted on the interstate highway, but because Mr. Potts was forced to stop so frequently for fuel, we kept catching up with him.

"Wouldn't now be a good time to radio for back-up?" I asked Congressman Narf.

"What, and share the glory?" he replied. "I think not."

"Well, at least you could have told Miss Foster the truth," I chastised him. "I mean, parrots! How is that fair?"

"Fair has nothing to do with it, kid," Congressman Narf opined. "In this world, it's every man for himself."

"I thought you told me it was politics," I reminded him.

"Same difference," the congressman said.

This was not unlike the fundamental message of Daschell Potts's famous book, *Folderol,* although in Mr. Potts's book, the character in question was a duckling and his heart was not nearly so jaded as the congressman's. Now that I think about it, Mr. Potts's story had more to do with self-reliance than with beating the competition.

Suddenly, cutting in front of us without so much as

a flick of the turn signal, and with the skill of a seasoned NASCAR driver, a Pontiac Grand Prix slipped into the slot between us and the school bus.

Immediately I identified the driver: Emily Foster, part-time FBI.

Out of the blue, Congressman Narf was faced with a rival and Daschell Potts had some real trouble snapping at his heels.

The Quarry Within Reach

It was one of those moments in traffic when things are not going smoothly for anybody. Because of the aggressive response by the newspaper columnist driver of the SUV at his side, Mr. Potts found himself shunted off the highway to the back road to Overland Park.

Caught by surprise, Congressman Narf and I missed the exit and shot on past—well, we were doing all of twenty-five miles per hour, so maybe "shot" is something of an exaggeration. Anyway, the wily ex-con skidded onto the shoulder, looking for a way to double back on the interstate, a move that is as suicidal as it is illegal.

Characteristically, Miss Foster was traveling so fast that she noticed nothing but a passing blur and, for all I knew, was destined for Des Moines. If so, I had no doubt she'd be there soon.

Meanwhile, back at the Ramada Inn in Conway, there was trouble in the lobby. (As the astute reader will recall, a common occurrence.) Duane had come to pick up Julia, all right, but he had brought his cheerleader friend Christine with him.

"Why is she here?" Julia asked, her voice as chilly as the interior of Superman's secret cave.

"We thought you had drownded," Duane explained.

"It's *drowned*, not *drownded*, you simpleton," Julia snapped. "And no, I didn't. I'm captain of the swim team, remember?"

"Well, that's what everybody said," whined Duane as Christine put her comely arm possessively around his football player's rock-hard waist. "Life goes on, you know."

"I wouldn't count on it, if I were you," fumed Julia. "Anyway, as long as you two are here, I'll let you take me home. Wait here while I get Jim."

"Who's Jim?" Duane asked.

But Julia had already disappeared around the back.

When she reappeared, Duane burst out in protest, "Jeez, Julia, he's not even of our species! You've got a lot of nerve getting all hissy about me and Christine."

"Oh, shut up and drive," Julia said, forcing her way into the back seat of Duane's Oldsmobile Cutlass with the friendly, overgrown, and aromatic ferret.

Things were not much better at the Mac Tonight McDonald's in Overland Park. Due to unusually heavy sunspot activity, the french fry computer had crashed and there was no telling when the problem would be fixed.

Animal control officer Taffy Malone found herself standing in a long line of impatient customers, some of whom kept looking at their watches the way people do at airline ticket counters, as if that's going to make any difference to anybody in charge. Taffy Malone passed the time by studying the restaurant's nutrition information, printed in tiny type on a flimsy little pamphlet, and available upon request.

My stars! She thought. *I never knew that a McDonald's biscuit with sausage and egg contains more than 500 calories, 33 grams of fat, 10 grams of saturated fat, 260 micrograms of cholesterol, and more than 1,200 micrograms of sodium, and that's before you sprinkle on the salt. Oh, but wait, there is a single gram of fiber. That's helpful.*

What Taffy Malone did not realize is that she had just discovered the motive behind Daschell Potts's killer ferret plan. Just as he had attempted to do so long ago with the publication of his landmark novel, *Folderol,* so was he now attempting with his busload of out-of-control ferrets.

Like me, and others of whom I've heard, Daschell Potts was a man on a noble mission: He was trying to save the world.

That the ferrets had snacked on a few miscellaneous clerks and cleaning ladies en route to Overland Park was unfortunate, and Mr. Potts truly regretted each and every one of the incidents, especially the inadvertent abandonment of so many pairs of perfectly good shoes, but the fact was that he'd trained the unruly animals to eat the high-calorie, high-cholesterol food so prevalent at McDonald's, not the customers, thereby hoping to save a hungry world from death by fat.

Alas, there is many a slip 'twixt the cup and the lip, and the best-laid plans of mice and men gang aft aglay. In other words, Mr. Potts was as much of a victim in the current scenario as all of the rest of us.

The ferrets had taken over.

Congressman Narf and I were back on Mr. Potts's

trail, noting that at one particular intersection near an abandoned air force base, a ferret had apparently bailed out through the bus window to devour the driver of a black Mercedes-Benz. Nothing remained but a turtle-waxed car and a pair of highly polished Johnston & Murphy shoes.

For those still keeping track of coincidences, the victim turned out to be one of the many claimants to the invention of the McDonald's Happy Meal, en route to his corner office at the top of a high-rise building in midtown. Since he was never on time for any meeting, it was six hours before police were called to the gruesome scene.

I must confess to a fundamental discomfort in reporting on the violence that large feral ferrets inflict upon our homeland. My personal sensitivities are elsewhere, I assure you. I'd prefer to describe the migration of butterflies through sunflower fields, or the purring sound a well-fed kitten makes when it rubs against your leg. But such diversions would be a betrayal of the trust that the writer establishes with the reader. I can only commiserate with you about the violence. I am powerless to stop it.

When Congressman Narf and I sputtered through the sod farms south of Leawood, Kansas, we caught sight of Mr. Potts's yellow school bus stopped at the railroad crossing up ahead. A one-hundred-and-fifty-car coal train from Wyoming was rumbling down the tracks to a high-polluting power plant in Georgia.

"Now's our chance," Congressman Narf announced.

Carnivore Caravan

A hundred yards from the railroad crossing and the yellow ferret-filled school bus, our battered Datsun pickup ran out of gas.

"Dang!" Congressman Narf complained. "I thought these things could go forever."

"Maybe there's a gas station nearby," I said optimistically.

"Yeah, and maybe there's a tanker truck pulling up behind us," Congressman Narf snarled. "Wise up, kid. Besides, I'm broke."

I looked out the back window. Incredibly, a Conoco truck was just pulling up behind us.

I hopped out of the cab.

Even from this distance, I could hear the music

blasting from the school bus. It was Ray Charles singing "Unchain My Heart."

"Can you spare maybe fifteen gallons?" I asked the driver of the Conoco truck.

"That depends," he replied. "Got any money?"

"I have this," I said, reaching into my pocket and pulling out the gold coin that Julia and I had found in the cave.

"What is it?" the driver asked.

"Pirate gold," I explained. "It's worth a fortune."

"Lemme see," the driver, nobody's fool, insisted. "Who's the goofball with the burger-eating grin on the heads side?" he asked suspiciously.

"That's Whitebeard," I told him. "The most wanted pirate in the whole sordid history of the Caribbean."

"He kind of resembles Ronald McDonald," the tanker truck driver observed.

"Except for a pair of big red shoes, what white man doesn't?" I replied.

The driver pondered the truth of my observation.

"Okay," he finally agreed. "But just fifteen gallons. Not a drop more."

"It's a deal," I agreed.

I returned to the Datsun to report my success to Congressman Narf.

"Amazing," he said. "Have you ever considered a career in politics?"

"I just want to stop the ferrets from hurting anybody else," I explained. "I'm sure they don't know what they're doing. Somehow Mr. Potts's attempts at conditioning them must have gone haywire."

"It's Potts who's gone haywire," Congressman Narf observed.

The last car of the cross-country coal train bumped noisily though the crossing. Daschell Potts drove his school bus across, his forty-nine remaining ferrets banging their knobby heads on the corrugated steel ceiling.

Soon, Congressman Narf and I were back on the chase, although Mr. Potts maintained a substantial lead.

The Conoco tanker followed close behind, inexplicably followed by a Pontiac Grand Prix piloted by none other than Miss Foster, who in turn was followed by an Oldsmobile Cutlass containing Duane, Christine, Julia, and Jim. Overhead, a lone great blue heron flew, keeping watch over our little parade.

Moses! I realized.

When the bus paused at a four-way stop near the Kansas-Missouri state line, three ferrets leaped out the windows and bounded toward the beer distributor on the corner. Although the receptionist was not spared—her gold Prada slings being all that remained—within an hour in the warehouse, the escapees managed to subdue themselves.

Easily captured in their inebriated condition, they were promptly transported to the Kansas City Zoo, where to this day they are presented to a gullible public as rare Irish wildebeest.

But let us return to the chase.

At 135th Street, on which one would eventually find the Mac Tonight McDonald's, the bus turned left. Except for the Conoco truck, which presumably had legitimate business elsewhere, the rest of us followed at a discreet distance. With the windows down, we could hear the Ray Charles tune "What'd I Say?" as clearly as if we were sitting in a corner booth at Mobster Mario's High-Hat Lounge, listening to the vintage jukebox.

Meanwhile, at the McDonald's restaurant on 135th Street, the french fry computer deglitched itself and the twin vats of hot oil began to bubble back into action.

A cheer erupted from those who had assembled during the past hour waiting for a steaming scoop of the world-famous fries. In fact, the noise was so great that Eduardo, an assistant manager trainee, stepped over to the Mac Tonight player piano, the one with the giant moon-headed Ray Charles look-alike on the bench, and turned the volume all the way to max.

At that very same moment, a dirty yellow school bus lurched into the parking lot.

"Well, boys," Mr. Potts announced. "It's been a long time coming, but at last the moment has arrived."

"*Chi-chi-chi!*" chittered the forty-six remaining ferrets, clambering for the exits.

Inside the normally quiet restaurant, a fracas was forming over the distribution of the steaming fries. Even otherwise God-fearing, churchgoing midwestern folk who'd moved to Kansas from such places as Nebraska, South Dakota, and Minnesota, and who under other circumstances could be counted on to love their neighbor and speak such niceties as "After you" and "No, you go right ahead," began pushing and shoving and shouting insulting remarks to one another.

Such is the addictive power of the McDonald's

french fry, a fact well known to Daschell Potts.

Trained to avoid becoming involved in a citizen melee, Overland Park animal control officer Taffy Malone stepped away from the increasingly hostile crowd and gazed out the window into the bright prairie sunshine. What she saw caused her blood to freeze.

"Holy macaroni and cheese on a Lenten Friday!" she gasped. "This will be a day to remember."

Death Takes a Holiday

Our comings and goings in this world are not affected by the annual events so important to the people at Hallmark Cards. People are born on Christmas Day. Others, unfortunately, are singled out for that day to die. But to my way of thinking, there should be one day set aside for an international moratorium on mortality. Surely, one day out of the year, we shouldn't have to fear for our lives.

And yet, at the McDonald's restaurant on 135th Street in Overland Park, Kansas, giant, bloodthirsty ferrets were clawing at the door. Luckily, it was not all forty-six of them. Half a dozen had run over to the

IHOP, where they became distracted by a stack of pancakes, and a couple of others had slipped into a furniture store, where they promptly fell asleep amid the impressive display of the leatherette Barca-loungers.

An even dozen lit out for the woods, which wasn't easy, given the traffic, but they made it, nevertheless, and for that, on this particular day, we should all be grateful.

One, always a loner, took up residence on the ninth fairway at a nearby golf course, where for several months before his capture he single-handedly reduced the wait for tee times by a third.

By now, Mr. Potts's murderous retinue was reduced by half. Twenty-five mustelid killers were pushing against a smudged glass door at McDonald's that clearly read PULL.

Though she did not single out Daschell Potts as the perpetrator, his menagerie did not go unnoticed by Overland Park animal control officer Taffy Malone.

Years before, when she first joined the force, Taffy Malone had been issued a sidearm, a Colt .38-caliber revolver, your basic six-shooter. Except for mandatory practice sessions against paper posters printed with turban-wearing silhouettes, she had never fired the weapon. That she carried it at all says more about local government's fear of wolves, bears, and mountain lions than it does about the character of Taffy Malone.

As Congressman Narf and I leapt from the Datsun and those who were following us searched for parking spaces in the crowded lot, Mr. Potts pulled open the door and twenty-five giant ferrets streamed into a noisy McDonald's, where the atmosphere was rich with the aroma of boiling, heavily salted french fries, grilled ground beef–like material, and melted processed cheese known in some circles as "cheese food."

Throughout history, every crisis has produced its hero. Think of Rosa Parks and her refusal to move to the back of the bus in Montgomery, Alabama. Or the anonymous Chinese youth who stood defiantly as the tanks bore down on him in Tiananmen Square. Think of George Washington crossing the Delaware in the dead of winter, his woolen socks frozen to his feet. Think of the now senator Hillary Rodham Clinton not murdering her husband when not only did she have the chance, but it was clear that no jury of her peers would have convicted her. Think about my mother and my father, who, after consuming a bottle of sweet Asti Spumante, agreed to bear a child—me.

Officer Taffy Malone was such a hero.

She rose to the occasion.

Before a single ferret could sink its teeth into a single McDonald's customer, Overland Park police officer and animal control specialist Taffy Malone fired her gun into the air, and the bullet struck a ceiling sprinkler system dead-on.

Immediately, the crowd went silent.

Suddenly, all that could be heard inside the restaurant was the player piano from the Mac Tonight room, still set on max, and playing the familiar melody to the timeless Ray Charles hit "I Can't Stop Loving You."

Highly paid psychologists spend years training rats to run in mazes for various superficial reasons. This is a process called conditioning. Something similar had taken place in the yellow bus as it lurched from Mississippi, through Arkansas, into Missouri, and to its present position in Kansas. Quite inadvertently, the ferrets had fallen under the spell of the timeless music of the legendary Ray Charles.

Like Catholic schoolgirls returning from recess, the ferrets filed one by docile one into the Mac Tonight room and gathered worshipfully around the piano, all twenty-five of them.

Meanwhile, the sprinkler system doused the formerly unruly crowd into complete submission.

It was a moment the likes of which could never have been predicted, but like coincidence, serendipity is a factor that has the power to change the course of modern history.

"Potts!" shouted Congressman Narf. "Surrender, sir."

"Not on your life," replied Mr. Potts, dashing out the door, pushing Julia and Christine aside and ejecting Duane from the driver's seat of the vintage Oldsmobile Cutlass. With one remaining passenger, my dear ferret friend Jim, Mr. Potts screeched out of the parking lot onto 135th Street and headed west at a dangerously excessive speed.

Eduardo, the assistant manager trainee, calmly walked over to the Mac Tonight dining room and closed and locked the door.

"These fries are soggy," complained a flamboyantly dressed woman who was something of a powerhouse in the real estate business.

"So are mine," said a nattily dressed man who

worked for a financial advisory service. "I'm not paying."

One by one, the wet-haired customers walked out as City of Overland Park fire trucks arrived, summoned by the alarm wired to the automatic sprinkler system.

I'll bet these guys will buy lots of coffee, thought Eduardo, who began firing up a big box-shaped coffee pot, once again proving himself to be the sort of management material that McDonald's top brass dream of.

An All-Glass Ferretorium

Emergency responders are the backbone of the security of this great nation of ours. The trained professionals who are first on the scene of a catastrophe literally make the difference between life and death for many thousands of people. Unfortunately, the same cannot be said for the fate of ferrets.

The members of the City of Overland Park Fire Department could extinguish a chemical fire, save citizens from burning buildings, stop a heart attack in progress, leap from a flaming tower onto a trampoline, and remove disoriented cats from thorn-covered trees, but when it came to dealing with a couple dozen giant ferrets temporarily contained in a glass-enclosed dining room, listening to preprogrammed piano music, the firefighters could only shut off the sprinkler system and throw up their hands.

"We could drown 'em," one suggested, the driver of the pumper truck, a short man named Max.

"That might ruin the piano," a fireman with a mustache pointed out.

"Heck, we could barbecue them all like hogs," another particularly hefty fireman volunteered, rubbing his prominent stomach and salivating at the thought. "I'll bet with a quart of sweet baked beans and tangy coleslaw they'd be plenty tasty."

"That doesn't solve the piano problem," his hirsute colleague reminded him. "In fact, it just makes it worse. You'd wind up melting that Ray 'Moonlight' Charles statue. And you know how expensive those things are."

"Well, then you tell me, Mr. Know-It-All," the fat firefighter countered. "You want I should call the pet adoption agency and find them all homes with little old ladies?"

"I'm thinking this may be one we should pass off to

the federal government," the mustachioed firefighter said.

"I'm glad you gentlemen agree," announced Emily Foster, flashing her FBI badge. "I'll take it from here."

"Hey, who wants coffee?" the fat firefighter asked his colleagues, relieved to be off the hook. "I'm buying."

With a happy smile on his face, Eduardo began filling Styrofoam cups. What with all the cutthroat competitive discounting in the fast food industry lately, McDonald's profit in a cup of coffee was equal to that from three regular hamburgers.

"So what's your plan?" I asked Miss Foster as Congressman Narf stepped into the free-coffee line.

"About that roomful of rats?" she replied. "Rat control is the restaurant owner's problem. I'm on the trail of giant parrots."

Meanwhile, out in the parking lot, Duane was sobbing uncontrollably.

"There, there, baby," Christine cooed. "It'll be all right."

"You don't understand," he blubbered, "I loved that car. That car was my life."

"I thought I was your life," Christine responded,

abruptly removing her arm from Duane's broad shoulders.

"You're part of my life," Duane cried. "But you're not the part that my car is."

"So what brings *you* here?" I asked Julia.

"Curiosity," she answered. "And other things."

Meanwhile, inside the restaurant, the manager was on the telephone with the owner.

"She says *we* have to handle it," he was explaining. "She says it's a pest-control issue. Yes, I saw her badge."

"Excuse me," interrupted Taffy Malone, "but perhaps I could be of assistance. I'm with animal control."

"Hold on, boss. There's a lady here who knows what to do," the manager reported. Handing Taffy Malone the phone, he added, "He wants to talk to you."

"If anybody needs me, I'll be at the Rainforest Café," Miss Foster said to no one in particular as she shoved her way out the door, inadvertently jostling the arm of Congressman Narf, who spilled his free hot coffee onto the fat fireman.

"Hey!" shouted the fireman. "Thanks for the lawsuit, nimrod."

With the familiar tune "Georgia on My Mind" starting up in the dining room, Eduardo's eyes grew large with fear.

"Uh-oh," he said to himself. "That's the last song on the tape."

When the Overland Park Police Department SWAT Team showed up, summoned, no doubt, by the owner of the hoagie sandwich shop down the street, Taffy Malone bravely went dashing out the door, waving her arms like a newly freed hostage.

"Back off, boys," she commanded. "This is an animal control issue. No need for the heavy artillery."

Frustrated by what seemed to be yet another false alarm, a few members of the highly motivated, pumped-up SWAT squad began randomly shooting out streetlights.

Later, the broken glass on the pavement would cause one of the fire trucks to have a flat tire, which, in turn, would delay its response to a legitimate call, resulting in the loss of the newly papered dining room of a lady who was entertaining a male associate with an intimate fondue party. She was able to save her lavish gated-community home by beating out the flames with a copy of Daschell Potts's *Folderol,* but she was unable to save either the dining room or the book, a rare first edition.

As Einstein only hinted at, for every action there is a successive and potentially endless string of undesirable reactions.

"I know what to do about those ferrets," I announced.

"Well, for goodness' sake," Taffy Malone replied, "this is no time for secrets. Tell me."

Daniel in the Lion's Den

I don't consider myself an especially brave person. But unlike some I could name, including one currently on the sidewalk, blubbering over the loss of his car, I'm willing to take my lumps and keep on going.

As my teacher said so long ago when she assigned me my personal motto, "Where there's a Will, there's a way."

The fact was, I knew these ferrets, the twenty-five remaining that were confined to the McDonald's glassed-in Mac Tonight dining room. Not that they were great friends of mine, mind you, but I'd come across many of them at Mr. Potts's house on the island. Although they'd growled at me, as I suppose they would at any intruder, they'd never actually attempted to eat me down to my shoes.

I also knew something of their recent history, and of Mr. Potts's possibly noble, possibly deranged, but ultimately incomplete efforts to condition the ferrets to seek out McDonald's highest-calorie food.

With the small crowd that remained in the restaurant—mostly firemen and police officers, with a few of the oddballs, idle hangers-on, literary agents, and newspaper reporters, that you get in any public place—I stepped up to the counter and addressed Eduardo.

"Twenty-six Big Macs, twenty-six supersize fries, and twenty-six large vanilla shakes, please," I said.

"Is that for here or to go?" Eduardo asked.

"For here," I replied.

"Why twenty-six orders," asked Julia, "when there are only twenty-five ferrets left?"

"You'll see," I assured her.

Meanwhile, Daschell Potts was making good time on the open road in Duane's souped-up Oldsmobile Cutlass. In fact, with Jim's nose out the window on the passenger's side, and the radio on, the writer and the friendly ferret were actually enjoying themselves, each feeling as carefree as a canary on the wing.

Slowly, in Mr. Potts's embattled mind, the fog began to lift and an idea of real substance began to form in its place.

"You know, Jim," he said over the sound of the wind and the radio, "it's easy to see why these wide-open spaces were so appealing to the pioneers."

"*Chi-chi-chi,*" replied Jim, shaking his head as a migrating monarch butterfly bounced off his pointed nose.

Eventually, somewhere not far from the community of Lyons, Kansas, they spied a hand-painted billboard at the junction of highways 56 and 14. CATTLE RANCH FOR SALE, it read. PRICE REDUCED FOR QUICK SALE. BRING YOUR OWN CATTLE AND NOTARY.

The sign pointed in the direction of Ellsworth.

"No harm in checking it out, I suppose," Mr. Potts said to Jim.

"*Chi-chi-chi,*" agreed Jim.

To Mr. Potts's surprise, along the way he saw a number of ranches that appeared to be devoted to species other than traditional Kansas beef cattle. Buffalo. Ostriches. Llamas. Burros. Kangaroos. A puppy mill specializing in a cross between poodles and Pomeranians, known as pomapoos.

THE PERFECT PET STORE PUPPY, the sign said. LOVE AT FIRST SIGHT.

There was even a ranch that raised nothing but prairie dogs.

"Now, there's one lazy son of a buck," Mr. Potts observed.

The ranch that was for sale turned out to be eighty well-watered acres adjacent to the prairie dog ranch. The price, by city standards, was a steal. The owner, a widow woman by the name of Mrs. Featherstone, had met a man through eHarmony and was anxious to move to St. Louis, where she intended to cohabit with the gentleman sight unseen.

"How often in a person's life does that person get to be with her perfect match?" she asked Mr. Potts.

"My guess would be never," Mr. Potts replied politely. "But I'm no expert."

Within fifteen minutes, Daschell Potts, using the *nom de real estate* "Cashill Dots" and a rusty notary stamp he'd found on the sandbar on the Mississippi, owned a plot of fenced land that was occupied by a single affectionate—although undeniably large—ferret.

As Mrs. Featherstone disappeared down the gravel

driveway, driven equally by high-octane gasoline and raging hormones, Mr. Potts named his new acquisition Dots Ferret Ranch Hideaway and B&B, and posted his enterprise in a flashy advertisement on the World Wide Web.

All of this happened in roughly the same amount of time that it took Eduardo to finish preparing my order for twenty-six of the biggest, fattest items McDonald's sold, and just as the Ray Charles tape sputtered out in the Mac Tonight dining room.

"Well," I said to Julia, picking up one of the twenty-six brown plastic trays. "I'm going in. Care to give me a hand?"

"That depends," she answered. "Can you guarantee that I won't be killed?"

"There are no guarantees in life," I told her.

Bravely, Julia picked up a tray and followed me into the lions' den.

While our backs were turned, and as I had known he would, Congressman Narf nabbed a tray for himself, ducking into a corner booth to scarf it down like a recently released federal prisoner.

You can take the con out of the penitentiary, but you can't take the con out of the con.

Circus, Circus

I never ran away from home to join the circus—the goal of many a young man only a couple of generations ago—but I did run away from home, and now I found myself in the center ring, so to speak, surrounded by twenty-five very large, unpredictable carnivores with my lovely assistant, Julia, occasionally by my side.

On the other side of the door, anxious faces of strangers were pressed against the glass, hand-held video cameras whirring, cell phone cameras clicking, and the mobile transmitter from KCTV-5 bouncing into the parking lot for a live shot.

Because of their downtown location, Channel 9 was running about twenty minutes late, and the crew from Channel 4, unfortunately, had gone to the wrong McDonald's, a midtown location, where they were taping an argument at the drive-through window about how many ketchup packets are supposed to be in a bag. To Channel 4's credit, they ran the footage anyway.

Carefully, so as not to get his arm bitten off, Eduardo slipped the trays of Big Macs, fries, and shakes to Julia, who, staked out by the barely opened door, calmly walked over and handed each one to me.

My method of distribution was based on the concept of medical triage. I fed the fiercest ferrets first, starting with the white ferret with the glowing red eyes. As I worked, I recited verses from Daschell Potts's classic novel, *Folderol,* in the most soothing voice I could muster under the strained circumstances.

"Paddle, paddle, paddle, your feet," I chanted, "slowly 'round the pond. Warily, warily, warily, warily, it all could be a con."

With information relayed through Julia, Eduardo instructed me how to restart the Ray Charles piano tape at the elevated Mac Tonight memorial. Within the first bars of "Crying Time," most of the ferrets were sitting down and quietly eating their meals. Through Julia, I sent word for a supplemental order of twenty-five hot apple pies. To heck with Congressman Narf, I figured. Let him get his own.

Meanwhile, the quick-thinking animal control officer Taffy Malone commandeered a laptop from a buttoned-down young man who'd lost his way to Starbucks.

In no time at all, Taffy Malone located a place in central Kansas called Dots Ferret Ranch Hideaway and B&B.

"Hello?" she said, when a man answered. "May I please speak to Dot?"

"You're talking to him, sweetheart," Mr. Potts said. "What can I do for you?"

Taffy Malone explained the situation.

"Sure," agreed Mr. Potts. "Bring 'em on. I can always use a few more ferrets. Will you be wanting a room for yourself?"

"I hadn't thought about that," Taffy Malone replied. "Perhaps I *should* make a reservation, just in case I'm running late."

This was a wise decision, because as it turned out, the ferrets were not anxious to leave, not so long as their favorite music was playing and high-calorie food was flowing through on plastic trays like manna from heaven.

Twenty-five soft-serves swirled with M&M's followed the pie order.

It was three hours before Taffy Malone, Julia, and I finally got the sleepy, overfed monsters loaded onto the abandoned yellow school bus.

By now, the SWAT team had removed its yellow crime scene tape from the parking lot and the guys from the City of Overland Park Fire Department had climbed back into their bright red trucks to respond to an actual emergency, this one a fire in a dumpster behind a Chinese restaurant down the road, an incident that was covered in excruciating detail by the late-on-the-scene Channel 4 News Team.

Leaving her roadkill-collection truck parked in front of the bank, Taffy Malone began the long and risky drive to a ranch somewhere south of Ellsworth, Kansas.

If ever the city of Overland Park decides to hand out a plaque for bravery, duty, and quick thinking on one's feet, I hope they give it to Taffy Malone. In fact, I wrote a letter to the city council making just such a recommendation. Unfortunately, it was set aside while council members debated the titles of the books permitted in public libraries.

"This *Huckleberry Finn,*" one outspoken member said. "It talks about African Americans in the most disparaging of terms. Let's ditch it, shall we?"

With a show of hands, the most famous Mark Twain novel of all time was relegated to the dumpster behind the Chinese restaurant.

"I'd like to bring up *Folderol,*" another member suggested, an officer with the local chapter of Ducks Unlimited. "It's insulting to waterfowl, in my opinion."

"Is that the Daschell Potts novel?" another, seeking clarification, asked.

"Yes, it is," the original complainer said.

"Well, goodness knows, he's a disagreeable man," the councilwoman continued. "Why should we hand over our hard-won taxes to the likes of him?"

"Good point," the chairman agreed.

"Julia," I said, after the last ferret had been safely boarded and was headed toward a new life on the ranch, "you are a real trouper. I have newfound respect for you."

"You're not such a bad guy, yourself, Will Finn," she replied. "Just a little quirky, that's all."

As tidy as this resolution seems, it was not what it appeared to be. Of the fifty man-eating ferrets Daschell Potts had put on his bus, only twenty-five were on their way to his overnight camp.

The others were still at large.

A Place in the Country

Many years ago, before McDonald's restaurants looked the way they do now, with bolted-down tubular steel and plastic booths inside, stunted non-native bushes outside, and truncated rooflines that attempt to present Americans' fanciful notions about English country cottages, the nation's leading ready-when-you-are eateries were strictly drive-through establishments—red and white tiled fried-fat huts floating in an oil-stained asphalt sea under a towering lighted image of a stick-man character with a round hamburger-shaped head.

His name was Speedy.

Often outlined in neon, this goofy, goon-faced character was balanced on one foot (as if running to your car with your order) atop a steel pole in the parking lot. In those days, the hamburgers he touted cost a mere fifteen cents.

The McDonald's version of Speedy closely resembled an equally fanciful and identically named character whose rounded goon-faced head was formed from a giant medicine tablet, a popular headache and upset-stomach remedy that fizzed when you dropped it into a glass of water. His full name was Speedy Alka-Seltzer.

I'm only speculating, but I imagine that the similarities between the two characters with the same name resulted in severe consternation in certain boardrooms and law offices at the time. That the issue was ultimately resolved with the creation of a tall, moronic white-faced clown is further evidence of the degree of corporate panic that must have prevailed during that era. Many people, especially children, fear clowns, and for good reason, I might add.

Ten thousand locations and thirty-some-odd years later, the crude and garish McDonald's manifestations of yesteryear are little more than a memory for a handful of frail senior citizens and a worthless relic in the Tchotchke Museum in Kansas City.

But here and there, from Florida to California, despite the determined efforts of a succession of blue blazer–wearing executives from the McDonald's Corporation, headquartered in Oak Brook, Illinois, a few of these early candy-striped eyesores have managed to survive. One restaurant even continues to present the original Speedy as if he had not been declared legally dead for more than a generation.

I suppose it's like trying to kill a vampire or a

werewolf. The dang things just keep popping up.

To those who have been following this narrative from the very beginning, it should come as no surprise that the throwback McDonald's in question is located, by a profound confluence of coincidences, near the long-suffering little town of Ellsworth, Kansas, the closest town of any consequence to Dots Ferret Ranch Hideaway and B&B. The reason that this outlaw McDonald's continues to operate is simply that no one other than the locals knows it is there.

Indeed, if ever you wanted to completely disappear, there is no more desirable spot on earth than somewhere along the back roads serving Ellsworth, Kansas. Now that I think about it, it's the very first place that I'd look for Osama Bin Laden, Jimmy Hoffa, and Amelia Earhart.

With a busload of lethargic ferrets, Overland Park animal control officer Taffy Malone had agreed to meet the man she knew as Cashill Dots, the pseudonym employed by famed author and ferret-crime abettor Daschell Potts, at that very Ellsworth-area McDonald's.

The meeting place, of course, was an obvious mistake on many levels, except for one: the one that has to do with the passions of the heart.

One look at the grizzled Mr. Potts, and the usually mature Taffy Malone found that her legs were reduced to Gumby limbs. One whiff of the pheromones emitted by the roadkill-scented body of Taffy Malone, and the hard-boiled Daschell Potts felt like a twelve-year-old staring at his sixth grade science teacher's partially revealed bosom.

It was, as they say, love at first sight.

Bluebirds twittered in the trees.

Bambi drank water from a still blue pond.

Neither of the adoring participants made much of an effort to contain the immediate mayhem that broke out when the twenty-five bus-riding ferrets stormed into the frozen-in-time Ellsworth-area McDonald's. Kids will be kids, after all, and ferrets, likewise, they tacitly agreed, will be ferrets.

Coming briefly to their senses, the two infatuees cooperated in rounding up their charges and drove them to the Dots Ferret Ranch Hideaway and B&B, where the animals were set free to terrorize the prairie dogs that, for that afternoon, and that afternoon only, lived next door.

Taffy Malone never returned to Overland Park to pick up either her roadkill-scooper truck or her commendation from the city council.

Life, in all its complex combinations, goes on.

All's Will That Ends Will

Love suited Daschell Potts.

In fact, it was from his serendipitous encounter with former Overland Park animal control officer Taffy Malone that Daschell Potts ultimately published his supreme work, the one for which he will be remembered through the ages: *Dead and Remarried*.

Not that was *Folderol* was forgotten, but it had finally been eclipsed by the only man with the talent to do so.

Many years later, when the Nobel Prize committee met in Stockholm, there was no debate. *Dead and Remarried* won the world's highest award for literature, hands down. The only problem was finding an address by which to notify the author of his million-plus-dollar prize.

It was also around this time that Congressman Pierre "Hercules" Narf accepted a teaching position at the Figure of Speech Academy of Modeling and Broadcasting in Memphis, Tennessee, where he supplemented his income by stealing printed matchbooks that he sold by the case on eBay, mostly to activists in third-world countries who had no imprinted matchbooks of their own.

He also moonlighted as a lobbyist for the owners of the *Memphis Empress,* the accident-prone riverboat excursion that recently had been cited for a variety of safety infractions by the National Transportation Board. With Congressman Narf's powerful connections, the company eventually paid a token thirty-dollar fine, based on ten dollars per confirmed drowning, and installed a hand-painted sign near the back reading ATTENTION: RIDE AT YOUR OWN RISK.

Duane never recovered his car. A well-meaning officer with the Overland Park Police Department told him he was lucky that he hadn't been conked on the head, a method favored by carjackers throughout the region. He suggested that Duane call a cab, even though the last time an available cab had been spotted in the southern suburbs of Kansas City was before Duane was born. Taking matters into his own hands, Duane instead hot-wired the roadkill truck that Taffy Malone had abandoned at the bank.

Once he got back to Marmaduke, Duane's family dined like kings for a week.

Christine, having walked to the shoe store to use the telephone to call her mother, wound up catching a ride back to Marmaduke with the store's assistant manager, a young immigrant with a visa issued in France, named Jacques Therapy. Despite the long drive, the two of them have been dating ever since.

The hardscrabble Good Samaritan driver of the turnip truck turned out to be right in his assessment of my insisting that Jim be permitted to ride in the back. Much to the old man's disappointment and serious financial loss, nobody would buy a turnip that smelled like a ferret's butt. I feel bad about that, but it isn't the only wrong decision I've made in my short life, so I am destined to live forever with the guilt.

Miss Foster never found her giant parrots, but she did receive a free piece of cake and a round of song at the Rainforest Café when she happened to mention to the waiter that it was her birthday.

The Kansas City man who falsely claimed to have invented the Happy Meal, who also developed the ill-attended Tchotchke Museum, bought the previously deserted sandbar south of Memphis and erected a thirty-six-story high-rise condominium tower on it. He named it after himself, of course, and added many millions of dollars to his already immense fortune. Everything comes at a price, however, for one day, when walking his property with his team of lawyers, a giant ferret leaped out of the bushes and bit off his ring fingers, of which he had more than most people.

My parents were happy to see me and quit quarreling as soon as I returned home. So far, things have been relatively peaceful, except for an occasional exchange of icy stares between them when they think I'm not looking.

Oh, well. When it comes to families, nobody's is perfect.

A few months later, Julia's family decided to heck with life in little Marmaduke. Julia's dad got a job running a Bed, Bath & Beyond store, and her mother is a crowd estimator for shopping plaza grand openings. They live in a brand-new three-bedroom townhouse near a four-hundred-acre nature preserve in south Overland Park.

I see her almost every day.

Together, Julia and I formed a volunteer afterschool service to find the twenty-five missing giant killer ferrets. We call our enterprise Children for Compassionate Capture. I know it's corny, but business, as they say, is business. Although we haven't found any of the runaway ferrets yet, we know it's just a matter of time. Not a day goes by that we don't see empty shoes in the road.

THE END